A LIGHTER SHADE

OF

GRAY

A LIGHTER SHADE OF GRAY

DENNIS JUNG

CITIOFBOOKS, INC.
3736 Eubank NE Suite A1
Albuquerque, NM 87111-3579
www.citiofbooks.com
Hotline: 1 (877) 389-2759
Fax: 1 (505) 930-7244

Ordering Information:
Quantity sales. Special discounts are available on quantity purchases by corporations, associations, and others. For details, contact the publisher at the address above.

Printed in the United States of America.

ISBN-13:	Softcover	979-8-89391-111-4
	eBook	979-8-89391-113-8
	Hardback	979-8-89391-112-1

Library of Congress Control Number: 2024909649

OTHER BOOKS BY THE AUTHOR

"A Lighter Shade of Gray" by Dennis Jung

"I don't see my heart as black. It's more like gray.
A sort of light shade of gray."

Black and white colors often represent light and dark, good and evil. Supposing that black represents the absence of light and white is regarded as the absence of darkness, how is white stained with darkness classified?

If criminals are judged as emotionless, black-hearted, cold people and those with good intentions are viewed as pure, white-hearted people. Lilly DeFranco, the protagonist, resembles the shade of gray and stands between white and black, neither good nor bad.

"A Lighter Shade of Gray" by Dennis Jung is an appealing fictional story focused on Lilly DeFranco, a fearless escape from the prison of Arizona in her search for redemption. (The Uneven Surface of the Soul). In her new start in Mexico, she finds herself employed as a bartender and becomes the trusted personal courier of Jeronimo Hermosa, a local crime boss. When Hermosa was approached by Hattie Rainer, his former lover, asking for his help to rescue their granddaughter Kate from her boyfriend, Leroy Burns, a gang member, he entrusted Lilly to deal with the matter, accompanied by Soledad. Their efforts quickly go awry after a violent encounter with Leroy and the police.

As the plot unfolds, the readers may ask: How do you entrust your loved ones to someone who gets their hands dirty? How far will you get your hands dirty for someone? After two months, Kate left a message in a diner in Villa Grove, stating she was ready to go home. Lilly and Solomon are on their quest again to retrieve her, where the readers will meet the greatest threat, the Daltons. Lilly is increasingly determined to rescue Kate from making the same mistakes that led her down the path of criminality, but to do this she must revert to her old ways. After having Kate back, Hattie's words to her, *"You can't let what happened in the past define you,"* inspired Lilly to believe that it is not too late to seek a lighter shade of her heart.

The author's use of visual imagery and a strong sense of place make her novels as much an escape from a geographical location as the mental landscape of the characters. The author often recycles his characters; thus, to know more about the protagonist's story, the readers must also read his earlier works. As suggested, to keep the audience glued to the story, more action, drama, and suspenseful scenes are needed. The plot is intriguing and exciting, and the characters are remarkable.

Lilly's toughness inspires the readers and those who have stumbled, chewed in, and spit out a couple of times to rise again and leave the past behind. A Chinese story, "Un cuento Chino" mentioned in the book, means that life has a lot of blind curves and unexpected developments, and her quitting the job involved with crimes is one unexpected development. This story is a strong testament to the possibility that someone can always turn back against their wrongdoings. Just like Lilly, she recognized her moral shortcomings, accepted her past, and walked to a lighter shade of gray.

TABLE OF CONTENTS

Dedicated to those of us who out of circumstance, misjudgment, or lack of choice, crossed the line and are at least cognizant of our failings.

ACKNOWLEDGEMENTS

I must first thank my wife Kathleen for her continued support, editing efforts, and tolerance. I extend my appreciation to my brother Steve for his valuable feedback, to my sister Katie for her encouragement, to Meg for her valuable critique. I also wish to thank Meredith, Tres, and Marv for their work on the cover photo. And finally, to my friends who encourage me to persevere in spite of my failing eyesight.

Author's Website Address: dennisjung.com

FOREWORD

By the time I had rewritten and edited my previous novel, THE UNEVEN SURFACE OF THE SOUL, for what seemed the hundredth time, I felt I had given short shrift to the character of Lilly DeFranco. I often recycle my characters, that is, I continue their sagas in subsequent stories. The character of Harlan Quist made his third appearance in THE UNEVEN SURFACE OF THE SOUL as I realized the arc of his story deserved such. I felt the character of Lilly DeFranco deserved nothing less.

More than a few of my protagonists are what I like to refer to as gray characters. By that I mean these are individuals whose moral compass often times aligns neither black nor white, but somewhere in between. Their personalities and codes of conduct were shaped by their background and experiences. Many faced adversities that at times left them broken, yet they endure.

Lilly Defianco is one such individual. As the title of this story suggests, she recognizes her moral shortcomings, accepts her past, but seeks to achieve a lighter shade of gray. She is a flawed femme fatale, an outlaw struggling to find her way in a world that seems to keep pulling her back.

This story is the second installment of a trilogy which will chronicle her search for redemption. I hope you enjoy the journey so far.

-Santa Fe, May 2024

PART ONE

"The first step toward becoming a true outlaw is the refusal to be victimized."

- Tim Robbins

Still Life with a Woodpecker

MEXICO CITY
January 2024

The driver pulled up in front of Jeronimo Hermosa's house at precisely six thirty pm on a cool winter evening. Hilario was the only name Lilly knew the driver by. He was an elderly *Indio* that had served Hermosa and his family since Jeronimo's childhood. Since Jeronimo was well into his seventies, that meant Hilario had to be at least in his eighties or nineties.

In contrast to his wrinkled, tobacco-colored face, Hilario's hair remained thick and coal black. He wore it long and pulled back into a braided and tightly coiled ponytail. As was his custom, the old man always wore an ill-fitting black suit with wide lapels that was shiny with wear. Jeronimo once speculated to Lilly that the suit predated his own birth.

Hilario raised a scabrous hand to tilt the rear-view mirror to meet Lilly's eyes. With a subtle nod of his head, he acknowledged their arrival. As was his manner, he meticulously placed the Mercedes in park and switched off the ignition and then slowly and laboriously climbed out, straightening his suit before opening Lilly' door.

"*Señorita,*" he croaked and offered a curt bow.

"*Gracias,* Hilario," she replied, taking his proffered hand.

She paused a moment to survey the estate's manicured grounds. The evening had grown quite cool and the air was heavy with the smell of wood smoke, for many of the residents in this neighborhood still favored fireplaces. The fading daylight softened the leafy grounds and contours of the Hermosa ancestral home. The mansion was situated in the Miguel Hidalgo neighborhood and bordered the Bosque De Chapultepec. From the driveway, a break in the tall conifer trees allowed a view of the looming edifice of the Chapultepec Castle.

As she made her way up the steps to the portico, she grimaced at the stitch of pain in her left thigh. Her femur had been shattered seven years prior and had never healed well, thus leaving her with a slight but still noticeable limp. This was in no small part to the inept orthopedic surgeon who had repaired her fractured femur in Arizona. The doctor had been contracted by the prison, and Lilly had always suspected he was an incompetent drunk. The damp evening air only served to aggravate the injury. Of course, the thirty minutes she had just spent on the treadmill at the gym hadn't helped matters either.

As she approached the portico, she spotted a figure standing in the shadow of a large potted fig tree. It was a man holding a shot gun loosely at his side. Even though he was half Hilario's age, his shoulder-length hair was shot with gray. He had a chiseled, weathered face and wore a blue tracksuit and black silver-toed cowboy boots.

"*Buenos Noches, Alfonso,*" she said with a nod. "*¿Como está tu esposa?*"

"*Ella está bien. ¿ Y tú?*"

"*Bien.*"

He leaned past her to open the massive wooden front door. Maria, Jeronimo's young house servant, greeted her at the door, no doubt expecting her. She too looked more *Indio* than *mestizo,* her heritage made more obvious by the elaborately embroidered *huipil* she always wore. She nodded a demure greeting and led Lilly down the wide, high-ceilinged hallway.

The last of the early evening light leaked through a large canopied skylight that ran the length of the hallway. In contrast to the mansion's colonial-styled exterior, the interior reflected more the taste of some Scandinavian timber baron – the molding and wainscoting done in polished, blonde teak. The hallway's Venetian-plastered walls were finished in a very pale yellow and accentuated by a mosaic of panels consisting of various colored and shaped tiles of translucent glass. A row of large aviaries lined one wall, and as they passed by, a chorus of bird song from a cage of finches announced their approach.

Lilly paused momentarily to offer a cautious finger to a large, brilliantly colored scarlet macaw perched on a bare tree branch in an open vestibule. She heard Maria behind her, clicking her tongue in disapproval.

"We have an understanding, don't we, Bruno? *Un entendimiento.* ¿Si?" Lilly whispered to the bird. "You bite, I bite. ¿Si?" She turned and followed Maria down the long hallway.

Jeronimo's father, a wealthy banker, had inherited the house from his father who had made his fortune in cattle and Yucatan sisal. At first, Jeronimo had embraced the family enterprises, going so far as pursuing an undergraduate degree in economics from Rice University and then a graduate business degree from the University of Texas in Austin. While studying there, he had cultivated a taste for a more libertine lifestyle.

He returned home soon after his father's death and promptly turned his back on the staid upper class *Chilango* world he grew up in and began to dabble in high risk, and not always above board, real estate schemes. He quickly realized his head for business dovetailed quite nicely with the city's burgeoning appetite for distractions, especially among Mexico City's *nouveau riche.*

He began purchasing restaurants, night clubs, and partnerships in the growing casino industry. As his reach into those endeavors grew, he found this gray world more to his liking. He soon found it easy enough to expand his interests into providing risky, high interest loans to entrepreneurs of less than stellar reputations and backing questionable real estate deals. From there, he migrated to bribing public officials, influence peddling and money laundering for certain select clients. Soon enough, no form of criminal enterprise or graft was off the table except for prostitution and drugs, his opposition to these enterprises based as much on practicalities as his often-Puritanic moral code.

Shortly after Jeronimo had hired Lilly, he, in a curious display of candor, related his curriculum vitae to Lilly. His openness was in response to Lilly's recounting of her own open litany of transgressions, including how she had ended up doing five years in an Arizona prison for armed robbery. Out of caution, she withheld telling him about her orchestrated escape from prison and the subsequent events that led her to seek refuge in Mexico City. He accepted her claim that she had come to the city looking for a second chance.

How she had risen to the position of his personal courier in less than a year had been partly the result of serendipity and partly due to her aptitude for recognizing opportunity. Soon after arriving in Mexico City, she had found a job tending bar in one of Hermosa's clubs that catered mostly to American tourists and expatriates. Outside of the idle gossip of her fellow employees, she knew little of her employer's criminality or his stature in the hierarchy of Mexico City's underworld.

One night while Lilly was cleaning the bar before closing, she inadvertently witnessed the club manager concealing two briefcases in the club's storeroom. After he departed, she gave into her curiosity and looked inside the briefcases only to find them stuffed with packets of white powder. Cocaine, she guessed, but for all she knew it might be heroin or fentanyl. One of the cases also contained bundles of pesos and US currency. She already had become aware that the manger had been skimming money. So she decided to take a chance.

Early the following morning, she appeared unannounced at Jeronimo's home to report what she had witnessed – both the drugs and the skimming. Jeronimo immediately dispatches several of his men to deal with the problem. Jeronimo was so impressed by her honesty and initiative that he offered Lilly the club manager's position.

That was a year ago. She steadily worked her way into Jeronimo's circle of trusted employees and soon became his courier and gofer. She never stopped marveling at this turn of events and her good fortune. Once a fugitive from both the US authorities and the Sinaloa cartel, she had now found refuge in Jeronimo Hermosa's patronage.

Maria opened the door to the study without knocking. The room was no less modern in its decor and furnishings. The walls were clad entirely in light brown teak with darker walnut accents. One wall displayed a large and elaborately painted depiction of Mayahuel, the Aztec goddess of the Maguey plant. The opposite wall displayed a pair of large Persian silk rugs.

The study's rear wall consisted of several immense glass sliding doors that opened on to a large solarium, its dominant feature a twenty-foot-high wall of black lava studded with dozens of orchids and stag horn ferns. The walls on either side of the solarium were adorned with large carved stone images of various Aztec deities.

The study itself was Spartan, its spare furnishings consisting of nothing more than a modest- sized leather and teak sofa, a large Afghani Kilim, and a glass-topped desk the size of a dining table.

This was where Jeronimo Hermosa sat peering at a large computer monitor. He raised one hand in greeting without taking his eyes off the screen. It was only when Lilly had dropped onto the sofa to wait that she noticed the man standing in the solarium. His back was turned toward the study, and he was leaning forward as if to smell an orchid. He was dressed entirely in black, his profile almost blending in with the dark lava rock.

"Good evening, Lilia," Jeronimo said, redirecting her attention. He cast a critical eye at the sight of her in gym clothes.

"I was at the gym when you called. You said it was urgent," she explained, aware of his unspoken, pedantic edict that women in his company be dressed in at least a semblance of decorum, Maria being the sole exception. As for his own attire, he usually preferred expensively tailored sport coats and slacks and always a crisp white dress shirt. This evening proved the exception, for he wore a rumple blue Oxford shirt with the sleeves rolled up to his elbows.

Jeronimo admitted to being seventy, although Lilly knew for a fact, he was edging seventy-five. He had a longish, fine-boned face beneath a stylishly coiffed mane of silver hair. His mouth was wide and generous with thin, aristocratic lips that rarely gifted a smile. Only his deep- set hazel eyes were ever allowed to display amusement.

He removed his glasses, tossed them onto a pile of papers, and sighed. "I'm sorry, but this is something that can't wait," he said softly with only the hint of an accent, although at times Lilly could often detect a drawl hinting at the years he had spent in Texas. "May I offer you something to eat? Some *cerviche*? Or perhaps some lettuce and carrots?"

She smiled, for she knew it was his way of mocking her newfound health food kick. "No, thank you. I'm fine."

"Tequila, then? Surely that isn't prohibited on your diet."

"Sure. Tequila's vegan. So, what's so urgent, *jefe*?"

Jeronimo removed a decanter of amber liquor from the desk cabinet along with a couple of crystal tumblers. He poured a generous amount in each glass and then stood and walked over to Lilly to hand her one before returning to his desk. He waited a moment as if lost in thought before picking up a large manila envelope at his elbow and slowly sliding it across to the edge of the desk.

"Inside you will find both of your plane tickets, hotel vouchers, two thousand US dollars and a name and address. You will seek out the person whose name I have provided and await her instructions."

"Wait. You said both. Who am I going with?"

He ignored her question, instead turning his attention back to the computer monitor.

She had never been accompanied on any of her previous courier assignments. Two or three times a month, she had traveled on his behalf to various cities in Mexico, twice to Rio de Janeiro, once to Cartagena, and at least a half-dozen times to Panama. Her duties entailed nothing more than personally delivering packages or letters, and then returning to Mexico City, sometimes with written replies, sometimes not. These tasks seemed simple and open. On the surface, they seemed to be business dealings with banks, hotels, restaurants, and the occasional assembly plant, and consisted mostly of delivering missives to secretaries and the occasional upper-level management type.

Only once had Jeronimo sent her to deliver a cryptic, spoken message. The recipient, an unsavory-looking gangster wannabe dressed in a cheap polyester suit met her outside of an outdoor market in Tepito, one of the city's sketchier neighborhoods. The message was simply, "*No cuelguestu ropasucia en public,*" What dirty laundry Jeronimo was referring to was never made clear. At first, the man received the message with scornful bravado. It was only when Lilly leaned closer and whispered, "*No te lo volverà a preguntar*" that his face registered apprehension. Telling someone that this was a final warning from *El Zorro Plateado*, the Silver Fox as Jeronimo was often called, always focused one's attention. She felt emboldened enough by this reaction to playfully pat his cheeks before smiling and strolling away.

When another long moment passed without a response from Jeronimo, Lilly took a swallow of her tequila and set the tumbler on a side table, knowing when to wait him out. Even though she hadn't known him that long, she had become used to his practiced, deliberate style of discussing matters.

"I will not lie to you, Lilia," he said finally. "This task may prove to be more difficult than your previous ones. It may present many complications and will require…"

He paused as the man who had been standing in the solarium stepped through a glass sliding door into the study. She recognized him, even though she didn't know him well. His name was Jaime Soledad, and he was also an American, a *Tejano* from South Texas. She knew second hand that he had been in Jeronimo's employ for six or seven years, but she still had no idea what role he served. They had encountered each other on a handful of occasions, but the actual number of words they had ever exchanged would fit on a gum wrapper.

Neither of them nodded a greeting. Soledad remained standing at the door as if awaiting an invitation to come in. She guessed he was in his late thirties. She had been told he was a *Chicano* despite his appearances, for he was what Mexicans referred to as a *Guero* - light-skinned and blonde. He had a smooth boyish face, was handsome, and knew it.

"I believe you know each other," Jeronimo said.

"We've met," she replied bluntly.

"Jaime will accompany you," he said, raising his hand as if to preempt her objection. He paused and started over. "This is a demanding situation. What you will be doing for me is something very personal. It has nothing to do with business. It is not the kind of thing I could ask any of my other people to do. It is a delicate task. A favor for an old friend, and one that will require discretion and, might I say, a woman's touch," he said, nodding at Lilly. "Nevertheless, it requires you both leave in the morning."

"Shit, *jefe,*" she said, giving into her irritation. "Can you at least tell me first where I'm going? Where we're going?" she added, correcting herself. She glanced at Soledad who hadn't moved from the door.

"You will go to Houston. I have booked you both on the six AM Aeromexico flight," Jeronimo said.

"ouston? Hold on," Lilly said, raising her hand in protest. "You want me to go the States? I thought you told me I would never have to go there. You said…"

"Come now, Lilia. You possess a valid passport. You will have no difficulty clearing immigration. I have also provided you with a visa and an entry permit. Everything is in order."

"You already got me a visa and a permit? Without even asking me first?"

"I must ask you first?" he said, his voice rising in obvious irritation.

"I'm sorry. It's just… I think they still have me on some watch list."

Lilia Montez was the name on her passport. It was a completely legitimate passport. The Minister of the Interior owed Jeronimo a favor and had personally facilitated the issuance. It had been backdated to appear it had been issued five years prior and bore plenty of entry stamps, just none from any US port of entry.

"I mean they've got all those fancy new facial recognition scanners. All it takes is for one of those immigration agents to pay attention and I'm screwed. What?" she asked in response to one of his rare and restrained smiles.

"There is no need to worry, Lilia. I have failed to tell you that shortly after you began your employment, I had my sources in the US do some investigating. This was done on your behalf as well as mine. I needed to know if there were any risks for me. And you should be happy to know that you are no longer on any such watch list. Your prison sentence was apparently commuted. Your criminal record expunged."

"You're kidding?"

She thought back to her last conversation with Davey Crockett, the ATF agent who facilitated the bounty payment she had demanded in exchange for handing over Gus Solomon, her former partner in crime. Crockett had attempted to entice her into returning to the States and testifying against Solomon in exchange for Witness Protection. When she turned him down, he reminded her that she was still a fugitive, for there was still the matter of her so-called prison escape and the ten years that remained of her prison sentence for armed robbery.

Crockett had either reconsidered or someone else had intervened on her behalf. She wondered if Crockett's operative and her former lover Harlan Quist had played a role. The last time they had seen each other he was being helped onto a helicopter, and she was about to flee into the night in a bullet-riddled Land Rover.

"You're positive I won't get flagged?"

"Positivo," he replied, dismissing her with a wave of his hand. "I assure you there will be no problem."

Lilly took another swallow of her tequila and glanced over at Soledad. "So do I get more instructions than that?" she asked, picking up the manila envelope and opening it. When Jeronimo didn't at first reply, she removed a slip of paper and read what was written there in Jeronimo's precise schoolboy handwriting. It simply read Hattie Ranier along with a phone number and directions.

"You mentioned once in passing something about Houston. I assume you know it?" Jeronimo asked her.

"No, not really."

She wasn't about to tell him that all she really knew of Houston were a couple of women's shelters, some cheap flop houses, and a half-dozen seedy bars out near the refineries.

"You said it was something personal? Tell me I'm not going all that way to deliver some kind of love letter," she said, not bothering to conceal her amusement. She had already learned just how far she could go with Jeronimo, but she didn't mind pushing the envelope so to speak.

"You are being impertinent, "he said with a sudden flash of anger. He held up his hands in frustration. "Look, if you cannot do this for me, I will find someone else."

"No. I apologize. I was out of line."

She took another swallow of her tequila, again waiting him out. He picked up his own glass, considered it for a moment and then set it back down. She could tell he was deliberating something. It was only when Soledad dropped on the sofa beside her that Jeronimo seemed to stir from his thoughts.

"Very well. I will cut to the chase as you are so fond of saying. When I was in graduate school in Austin… This was 1975. This Ranier woman and I became involved. *Romàntic omente.* Lovers, if you must know." He paused as if editing something in his mind.

"I proposed marriage, and I even brought her to meet my parents. She was too…. modern and liberated for such an arrangement is how she referred to marriage. Or so she said. So we went our separate ways, but we stayed in touch. She would occasionally come to Mexico City. I persisted in my efforts to wed her, and she continued to resist. At some point, she became aware of my business dealings. There was another woman I was involved with at the time. Out of spite and jealousy, I believe she revealed certain things to Hattie. Despite my best efforts, Hattie announced she would not see me again. Her moral code would not allow it, if you will."

He topped off his glass of tequila without bothering to offer any to her or Soledad.

"It has been thirty… No. Almost thirty-five years since we last communicated. This in spite of my efforts to reach her. My letters went unanswered. I had people attempt to find her, but nothing. There was no trace of her. I had put any thoughts of her aside until three days ago when she contacted me." He paused a moment before going on.

"She called me seeking my help." He shrugged. "You may ask what I could owe her after these many years. The wounds of the heart are not so easily healed though."

"And?" Soledad asked after a long moment had passed.

"It seems she operates what she called a halfway house in Houston for… wayward women are how she described it. Women on parole. Addicts, perhaps. She never went into specifics. There is a young woman… a resident or a guest as she called her. This young woman has run off, and Hattie feels she is in danger. Hattie and this young woman have a connection of some sort that…" He paused and started over. "She has tried several avenues to extricate this young woman from this situation in which she finds herself. The authorities are of no help. She has gone so far as to employ a private investigator who also was of no help."

"And she's asking you to do what exactly?" Lilly asked. "And why did she come to you?"

"Why? Because I am a criminal," he replied with obvious bitterness. He took a swallow of tequila before going on. "It seems this young woman has become the consort of the leader of a criminal gang. Hattie is afraid of involving the police in this matter because she does not wish the girl to be arrested. Or worse. Her own attempts to intercede have now resulted in death threats against her."

"What kind of gang?" Soledad asked.

"What is the word she used? Skin heads, *si?*"

Lilly snorted in amusement.

¿Qué?"

"Nothing. Just…" She shook her head. She was coming full circle. Thirteen years ago, she had been the lover and partner of the leader of a white nationalist militia in Idaho. She couldn't escape her past.

"And so you want us to find her and get her out of there?" Lilly asked.

"And protect her. And Hattie."

"If you're asking me to be a bodyguard, you should find someone else. That's not one of my talents."

She had never revealed any details about her abduction at the hands of her former bank robber partner Gus Solomon and her brief captivity in Sonora. Nor the revenge she had inflicted on Higinio Vargas, the cartel capo who had threatened to feed her to his pigs. Yes, she had met violence with violence, but that didn't make her a bodyguard by any stretch of the imagination.

"That is why Jaime will be accompanying you."

She glanced at Soledad who failed to meet her gaze.

"Okay. Sure, that sounds simple enough," she said without making any effort to conceal her sarcasm. "Is there anything else?" When Jeronimo shook his head in dismissal, she finished her tequila and stood up.

"I trust you with this, Lilia. That is no small thing. Trust. I have always found it a scarce commodity. Text me when you arrive. And then call me when you have something to report."

"Sure thing, boss," she said, scooping up the envelope from the desk and turning to leave.

Soledad stood and she sensed him following her out into the hallway. She turned abruptly, and he almost ran into her.

"So you're one of his *pistoleros?*" she asked, not making any attempt to mask her irritation

"No. I'm like you. Just an errand boy." He was soft-spoken with a bit of a drawl.

"I don't like this," she said, starting down the hallway.

"What? Me going with you?"

She turned again and looked at him. "No. Well, yeah. That and the fact that this isn't the kind of shit I signed up for. What he's doing, or should I say what he's asking us to do is a shit show. I'm guessing you didn't try talking him out of this."

"Are you kidding? I'm not that high up on the food chain. I'm surprised he let you get away with your attitude."

"My attitude?"

"Look, we go check it out. If this isn't doable, we tell him as much. I mean, what does he really owe this Ranier woman?"

"I'm starting to wonder what it is he thinks I owe him."

He shrugged. "So then why did you agree to do it?"

She did owe Jeronimo, but she sure as hell wasn't going to admit that to Soledad. "Okay, we go to Houston. No harm in seeing how far it goes," she said, starting to turn away.

"That tattoo of yours," he said, pointing to her bicep. "There's always a story behind ink like that," he said with no amusement in his voice.

The tattoo was that of an eagle holding a strand of barbed wire in its beak. She folded her arms, covering the tattoo with her one hand. She had gotten it soon after arriving in Culiacán after fleeing Idaho. It had been nothing more than a drunken celebration of life. Yes, there was a story, but not one she wished to ever share with Soledad.

"I'll meet you at the gate in the morning," she said and walked away, leaving him in the hallway.

Maria was nowhere to be seen, so she let herself out, but not before pausing to offer a peanut to Bruno the parrot. She nodded again to the man with the shotgun and made her way to the car. Hilario stood waiting for her at the bottom of the stairs with Mercedes' door open.

"¿Me *llevarás al aeropuerto por manana??*"

"*Como deséres, senorita.*"

Soledad could find his own way to the airport. She paused with one leg in the Mercedes and wondered if Hilario had known or remembered Hattie Ranier.

"*Dime, Hilario. ¿Conocías a* Hattie Ranier?"

The old man considered the question before nodding. "*Si. Ella es una bruja,*" he muttered, making a slow and deliberate sign of the cross.

"*¿Una bruja?* No shit? A witch."

This might prove interesting after all, she thought climbing into the seat. She should remind herself to bring some garlic.

S oledad watched Lilly stalk off. He had never noticed the limp before. Nor had h noticed the small crescent-shaped scar below her right eye, or the ridge-like crease on the bridge of her nose. It was a tell tale sign she had once broken her nose. Or someone had broken it fort her. He did remember that she was a nice-looking woman. The skin-tight leggings and sleeveless top left little to the imagination. He guessed she was fortyish even though her well-toned body might suggest she was younger. He also remembered that in the limited occasions in which they had shared close quarters, she had always seemed to project an aura of understated *machisma*. Something told him she might prove to be a handful on a job like this.

All he really knew about her was that Jeronimo used her as his personal courier for his legitimate business dealings. It seemed odd he would be entrusting her with something like this. Then again, she might fit the kind of low profile Jeronimo needed for what he had called a delicate task that required discretion. He assumed that the fact they were both Americans might mean they would attract less attention.

He slipped back into the study. Jeronimo glanced up at him before finishing what he was doing on the computer.

"I assume you have questions," Jeronimo said, pushing his chair back from the desk. "About this job? Or Lilia?"

Soledad cocked his head in reply. "Both, actually."

"I can tell you Lilia is not what she seems. Therefore, be careful not to underestimate her."

"Meaning what exactly? I already know she's hard to read. I gather there's more I need to know."

"There are certain things I know about her. Things she is not aware that I know."

"Such as?"

Jeronimo held out the bottle of tequila to Soledad who paused and picked up the tumbler Lilly had left on the side table. He took the bottle and before pouring a shot, held the glass to the light. He could see where Lilly's lips had smudged the rim. He held it to his nose and thought he could detect some scent other than the tequila. Cinnamon?

"You should know that she has what one might term a colorful past. A criminal past. Bank robbery, armored car robbery, amongst other offenses. *¿Cómo se dice?* What is it you police call such things? A record. A rap sheet, *si?* Yes, she has such a sheet going back to when she was quite young. She revealed that much to me after I hired her to take over the club. She admits to escaping from prison in Arizona, but I have an informant who believes that this escape was not what it seems. *¿Por qué? No sé.*" He shrugged. "Then there is the story of an American woman fitting her description being implicated in the death of a capo in the Sinaloa cartel. The story is that this woman fed him to his own pigs. As I said, Lilia is a complicated woman whose talents may not always meet the eye."

"Shit, *jefe,*" Soledad murmured.

"*Exactamente.* She is capable, but may require…How should I say this? Guidance and restraint."

"And this job? Am I missing something? I mean there must be more to it than what you've told us."

He didn't reply at first. "Just do it," he said quietly. "And don't ask questions. Understood?"

"Loud and clear."

"I chose the two of you because you each have certain talents. You will know what can and cannot be accomplished. You are level-headed I believe is the term."

"And her?"

"When there are women involved, a man may not suffice. You may not read certain things. ¿Lo *entiendes?* Here. You should have this," he said, handing him a slip of paper. "This is a contact in Houston who can provide you with certain resources if needed."

"Resources?"

"Additional surveillance. Weapons, if need be."

"Weapons." He shook his head. "I have to be honest with you, boss. I don't see a good ending to this. Say we manage to get this girl away from this gang. I doubt it's going to end there."

"Then you must make it end there. Do I make myself clear?"

"*Claro, jefe.*"

Soledad was beginning to realize this mission would be much more complicated than he first thought.

"Now leave me."

Soledad nodded, finished his drink and walked out. He felt a tinge of anticipation. Jeronimo hadn't entrusted him with anything like this for a good while. It was nothing like his usual problem-solving assignments. The job itself was only the half of it. Something told him that Lilia Montez, or whatever her real name was, would make it even more interesting.

HOUSTON

Jeronimo was right in reassuring her that immigration at Bush International wouldn't present a problem. The immigration agent had studied her documents before giving a cursory glance at the woman standing across the counter from him.

What he saw was an attractive, fair complexioned woman in her early forties. Her eye were large and round, the pupils a watery blue that seemed to accentuate the weariness evident in her face. She was stylishly attired in an ankle-length black wool skirt and matching blazer over a cream-colored blouse accentuated by a necklace of jade beads and a small gold figurine. The woman's dark auburn hair had been cut in a bob that complimented her delicate features. He must have concluded she certainly didn't look like your average drug mule, and without asking her any questions, stamped her passport and entry papers and waved her through.

She had purposefully dressed up in the hope she would avoid scrutiny by immigration. The gold pendant had been an afterthought. It was that of the Aztec goddess Coatlicue, a birthday gift from Jeronimo. A good luck charm, he had told her

She and Soledad had shared adjoining seats in the first-class cabin of the Aeromexico flight. They had exchanged small talk and curt pleasantries over breakfast, neither seemingly willing to openly discuss the details of their mission much less anything in the way of personal revelations. Lilly had cat-napped for most of the two and a half-hour flight, for she hadn't slept much the night before. Despite Jeronimo's assurances, she couldn't shake her anxiety about returning to the States. Houston especially held far too many unpleasant memories.

Eight years ago, she had arrived there in the middle of the night on a bus with two hundred dollars and the handful of jewelry she had managed to snatch before crawling out the rear window of her apartment in Culiacán mere minutes before a cartel hit team came looking for her. She had survived the streets of Houston by using only her wits and her bravado, and without the protection and resources women living that kind of life needed to evade the obvious pitfalls and perils. She had only escaped that existence with the aid of Gus Solomon, a violent sociopath who eventually proved to be her downfall. And yet, here she was returning to Houston while traveling in the lap of luxury. Life was strange that way, she thought as she waited for Soledad to pick up their rental car.

It was only nine in the morning, and they wouldn't be able to check into their rooms at the Westin until early afternoon. Their hotel was situated in The Woodlands, a popular, upscale suburb of Houston. It was also a part of the city favored by wealthy Mexicans. The directions to Hattie Ranier's place indicated it was in an area just north of The Woodlands. It seemed an unlikely place for a halfway house for drug addicts or parolees.

While waiting to board their flight in Mexico City, Lilly undertook an internet search to see if there were any hits on Hattie Ranier. It wasn't until the third page that she found a short article in the Houston Chronicle reporting that a settlement had been reached over a zoning dispute between The Woodland Township's Board of Directors and Hattie Ranier, the owner of the Zen Women's Refuge. A mediator had ruled in favor of Ranier, citing the fact that the three-acre plot of semi-rural land was located on county land and a was not in violation of any

Harris County zoning regulations. Furthermore, the mediator declared the refuge didn't detract from the development's appearance, nor did it present any threat to the residents. Oddly enough, Lilly couldn't find any other link to Ranier's name.

Soledad suggested they get the lay of the land and at least drive by Hattie Ranier's establishment since it was only a half-hour drive from the airport. A half-hour morphed into an hour due to a four-car pileup on the freeway. They had been creeping through the bumper-to-bumper traffic for perhaps ten minutes before Soledad broke the silence.

"You know we're going have to talk at some point. What I mean is that we might as well get comfortable with each other."

She looked at him but didn't say anything.

"Okay. So, what's your beef with me?" he asked.

"I don't have an issue with you specifically. It's just I've never had anyone go with me on any of my jobs. You should know I'm a bit of a lone wolf. I keep to myself. You could say I don't play well with others. My mother used to tell me that."

"Something tells me you were a biter in kindergarten."

She smiled at the memory of Harlan Quist accusing her once of being a biter as a child. She looked at him. "It's best you keep that in mind."

He nodded. A couple of minutes passed before he said anything. "I guess you already know I grew up here. Not in Houston, but in Texas. About three hundred miles south of here. My folks had what passed for a farm in Starr County. A stone's throw from the Rio Grande. I never left there until I turned eighteen and joined the Marines. I spent three years in Korea and came home to nothing. My folks had died, and the farm had been sold for back taxes. So, I moved to San Antonio and became a cop. I made it to detective before I was shit canned for taking a bribe. They couldn't ever prove it, so I was never charged."

"But you took it, didn't you? The bribe?"

He smiled. "You need to know some things about me, Lilia."

"It's Lilly, actually. And I really don't need to now."

He looked at her. "Yeah, I took it. Five grand to look the other way on a…. transaction. My old man used to tell me how if you weren't careful and took just one misstep in life, it'll set you on this path to perdition is how he put it. He was part time deacon and talked like that a lot. Turns out he was right," he said with a smirk.

"And once you're an outlaw, you're always an outlaw," she said.

"Are you speaking from experience?"

"Look, I don't know what Jeronimo told you about me, but I'm not the person I used to be." Or at least I like to tell myself that, she thought.

"I keep my head down and keep to myself. Okay? What I said about being an outlaw and that never changing. Well, I just want to stop running."

Neither of them spoke as they slowly cruised by an overturned tractor trailer and the charred and still smoking wreckage of a sedan.

"Tell me something," she said as they sped up to join the stream of now frantic traffic. "What is it exactly that you do for Jeronimo?"

"Human Resources," he replied with a straight face.

"So, you do the hiring and explain Jeronimo's generous benefit packages to prospective employees. So, I guess you also terminate people."

He offered a slight nod of his head. "Yeah, you could say so."

"Did you happen to be the one that terminated that club manager I ratted out?"

"As a matter of fact, I was. I offered him a severance package that consisted mostly of him catching the first stagecoach out of Dodge." He looked at her and smiled. "But what I mostly do is perform background checks and keep an eye on Jeronimo's employees. And sometimes on his competitors. I do a fair bit of surveillance. And like you, sometimes I deliver messages."

"Have you ever done anything like this?"

"No, nothing ever quite like this."

"So, we talk to this Ranier woman first. Get all the details. Then what?"

"Depends. We need to locate this young woman first. We do some surveillance to see what we're dealing with. Getting her away from whatever she's gotten herself into might be as simple as picking her up and bringing her back to Ranier's place. Or not."

"Say the girl doesn't want to go back. Say her boyfriend doesn't want to let her go. That means we might have to abduct her. And even if we bring her back, that doesn't mean she's necessarily going to stay. Like I said, this could easily turn into a shit show."

Soledad didn't say anything.

"What do you really make of all this? I mean Jeronimo and the Ranier woman. It doesn't make sense that she calls out of the blue after all this time and asks for this kind of a favor."

"All I can figure is she must've had her hooks in him. One of those kinds of women."

"And what kind is that?"

Lilly thought about what Hilario had said about Hattie Ranier. There must have been something about her that made quite the impression on the old Mexican.

"I guess we'll find out soon enough," Soledad said.

The GPS directed them to take the first exit off the I-45 to The Woodlands. The secondary road led them along a heavily wooded area. On one side were rows of expensive-looking houses on large lots, the yards of which were partially concealed by high wooden or brick fences. Thick brush and trees lined the opposite side of the highway except for the occasional more modest residences. Some of these plots had horse corrals and sheds containing tractors and farm equipment. They passed a new residential development, the partially completed houses more modest in size and acreage than those in The Woodlands.

After a mile or so, the GPS announced their destination lay just ahead. Unsure of the turnoff, Soledad slowed as he passed an older model delivery-type van parked on a pullover. There was a logo of some kind painted on the side, but it was too faded to read. The van's front fender appeared badly dented. He gave it a quick glance and sped up.

Some thirty or so yards further down the road they came upon a metal security gate. "You have reached your destination," the classy British-accented voice assured them. They didn't see a mailbox or obvious signage, but there was an intercom next to the gate. Soledad pulled up beside it and paused for a moment before pointing to something in a tree beside the gate.

"Security camera. You see it?"

Lilly leaned across him and nodded. Soledad punched the intercom button and a moment later a tinny sounding woman's voice answered with a simple yes.

"We're here to see Hattie Ranier."

There was a pause before the voice said, "Hattie? You mean Punna. She isn't available at the moment. Would you like to leave a message?"

"Punna? No, we're here to see Hattie."

"Yes, Hattie. Punna."

Soledad looked at Lilly and shrugged. She leaned across from him. "Tell Punna that Jeronimo sent us."

"Oh, yes. Geronimo. Like the Indian. Punna said you might be dropping in. Follow the road," the woman said and disconnected. A moment later, the gate swung open.

A muddy road wound through thick stands of scrub oak and loblolly pine for seventy-five yards before ending at a grassy clearing. A small, graveled parking area sat in front of a large two-story brick structure. The parking lot sat empty except for a muddy, late model 4Runner and an old Nissan sedan.

Soledad pulled up next to the two vehicles and cut the ignition. The house didn't appear to be of recent construction because the brick in many places appeared weathered and eroded. A large wooden porch in serious need of painting encircled two sides of the house. In front was a well-manicured patch of lawn adorned by several pieces of some kind of stone statuary. A row of fallow shrubs lined the front of the porch. Lilly recognized some of them as roses.

They got out and walked across the sodden lawn to what appeared to be the front entryway. It was then that Lilly realized the statues depicted various representations of the Buddha. Some were merely heads; others were of the Buddha in a reclining or sitting position. A small fountain and pond containing some *koi* completed the garden.

A metal security screen cloaked a sturdy appearing wooden door. Glancing around, Lilly saw all the windows were also covered with ornate, heavy duty security grating. She found herself wondering if the screens were intended to keep someone from entering or from leaving.

Before they could ring the buzzer, the heavy wooden front door swung open. A slight, older woman with a shaved head and wearing denim overalls, smiled at them. She bowed her head in greeting and unlocked the security gate.

"Welcome," she said, stepping back to allow them entrance.

They stepped into a large room dominated by a massive fireplace at one end. The room appeared devoid of any furniture to speak of other than a dozen or so large throw pillows and an expensive-looking Oriental rug that covered most of the wooden floor. The walls were painted a light green and adorned with a dozen or so small, elaborate tapestries depicting images of the Buddha. *Thangkas*, Lilly thought they were called. She had once seen some in an exhibit of Asian art at a museum in Mexico City.

"Please remove your shoes if you don't mind. We don't allow them in the house," the woman explained. Her accent sounded Germanic. "Punna will be down shortly. She had some business to attend to. You may sit," she said, gesturing to the pillows. "Or stand if you are more comfortable."

There was a sudden clanging noise from the back of the house. It sounded like pans rattling. Looking past the woman, Lilly caught a brief glance of a woman hurrying across the open hallway into another room.

"Lunch preparations," the woman with the shaved head explained. For the first time, Lilly noticed a tattoo of some sort snaking up from beneath the collar of the woman's frayed jersey. She appeared to be sixty or so with coarse features and steel gray eyes. The wrinkles around her mouth suggested a lifetime of smoking.

The woman nodded and disappeared down the hallway. Neither of them made a move to the pillows. The air was heavy with the smell of incense and what might have been curry wafting down the hallway from the kitchen.

'Punna," Soledad said, slipping off his boots. "That sounds sort of sexy if you ask me."

Lilly kicked off her flats and walked over to inspect one of the *thangkas*. It showed the Buddha sitting cross-legged in a meditative pose atop a snow-capped mountain and surrounded by mounds of flowers, lilies.

There were suddenly voices coming from the head of the stairs, and a moment later a morbidly thin young woman dressed in an ill-fitting smock made her way cautiously down the stairs, and after casting a curious glance at them, headed to the back of the house. Another moment passed before another figure appeared on the stairs. It was a tall woman wearing a burnt, orange-colored robe. Her head was also shaven, and she wore small, oval spectacles. She paused at the bottom of the stairs before moving into the living room. She looked at each of them in turn before smiling and clasping her palms together and nodding.

"Welcome," she said, lowering her head. She looked up at them and moved closer. "I take it you're … associates of Jeronimo." She glanced at Soledad. "You I can see," she said, taking in his jeans and black leather bomber jacket. "But you," she said, turning to Lilly. "You are something entirely unexpected."

She spoke with the kind of honeyed Southern drawl of someone who might have just stepped off the set of 'Gone with the Wind'.

"I'm Lilly and this is Soledad," Lilly said, extending her hand.

Punna aka Hattie took Lilly's hand in both of hers and gripped it tightly. Her hands felt roughened as if she spent a fair share of time working outside. She held Lilly's hand for longer than seemed necessary, all the while gazing at Lilly intently. She finally let go and stepped back without making any effort to shake Soledad's hand.

"I suppose you're wondering about the name. I chose Punna when I was ordained as a Buddhist nun. It means one who seeks kharma. Or at least a better kharma. But you can call me Hattie. Just please not around the guests."

"Guests? Tell me something," Lilly said. "Do they choose to come here or does their parole officer make them come?"

Hattie smiled. "They are given a choice of here or some dump in the Fifth ward. Better food here and far less distractions. After a week here, they realize how well off they are."

"Except for the one that ran off," Soledad offered.

Hattie looked at him. "Yes, except for her. Why don't we step into my office? It has chairs," she added and turned and led them into a side room. She closed the door behind them and dropped into a wooden swivel chair that was at least as old as the house.

"Would either of you like some tea? I don't keep coffee in the house. It was too often abused, and I do my best to keep the ladies on the calm side."

They both deferred. Lilly glanced around the office. There were four photos on the otherwise bare walls. One of the images displayed a smiling Dalai Lama. Another showed a group of Caucasian women in nun's robes standing beneath a huge banyan tree. On the opposite wall was a faded black and white portrait of an elderly woman in a rocking chair.

Beside it was a large and obviously professionally done photograph of a young woman astride a white horse. The photo had been taken on a beach. The woman wore a bikini and was leaning forward in the saddle to cress the horse's neck, her long black tresses spilling onto the horse's head.

The afternoon sun streamed through a side window allowing Lilly a chance to gain a better appreciation of Hattie's face. Her shaved head and age side, Lilly could tell Hattie Ranier had once been quite the beauty. She could envision her gliding down a wide staircase at some debutante ball. What were they called? A Cotillion, maybe? Something like that. For some reason, she had always liked the sound of that word. She had once heard it in a movie. It could've been 'Gone with the Wind'. She remembered they had shown it a couple of times at the prison in Arizona.

Hattie Ranier had startlingly blue eyes, perfect teeth in a wide, generous mouth, and the kind of facial bone structure whose image might grace a plastic surgeon's waiting room. Even her bare skull was elegant and perfect, her fine fuzz of silvery gray hair only adding to her appeal.

"So. My runaway. Her name is Kate. She turns nineteen in a month and was sent here because of a series of run-ins with the law. Misdemeanor thefts. Drug possession. She was arrested for carrying an ounce of marijuana. Resisting arrest. Carrying a false ID. She's currently awaiting trial for aggravated assault. She kicked a bouncer in the balls."

She earns three stars for that one, Lilly thought to herself.

"Her so-called boyfriend runs with a group of miscreants who call themselves the White Liberation Front. They're nothing more than Aryan Brotherhood wannabes. From what I can tell, all they really do is hold up liquor stores, deal in stolen guns, and torch the occasional black night club. I found all this out from an acquaintance who works at the Houston Police. She was able to look at the files of the HPD Gang Unit."

"And the cops can't help?"

"Sure. They could bust them and arrest her. I don't want to see Kate incarcerated. It would only fuck up her situation even more, pardon my French."

"What about her parole officer?"

"Worthless. He was supposed to check in with her here a week ago, but never even called."

"I imagine this has happened before. I mean residents skipping out," Lilly said. "What makes Kate any different?"

Hattie pursed her lips and hesitated before answering. "There's her potential for one thing. I know that sounds like a cliché, but she is an exceptional young woman, her drug habit and acquaintances aside. She was…" She hesitated. "Her records indicate she was a very precocious child with an extremely high IQ, but she dropped out of school when she was sixteen."

"But yet she gets involved with these scrumbags?" Soledad remarked.

"She's reckless. Street wise, but reckless. And headstrong."

"Any family?" Lilly asked.

"Her mother's deceased. Her father…" She shrugged. "Who knows?"

"So where do we find these guys?" Soledad asked.

"There's a house in the Northwest part of town. It's not that far from here. My friend at HPD found out there are a half-dozen of them living there. Ex-cons, neo-Nazis. Skinheads. Yeah, I know," she said, running her a hand across her shaved scalp. "But like you said, they're nothing more than low life criminals."

"And you're sure Kate is there?" Lilly asked.

"I know she's there. I tracked her cell phone. I even went there looking for her. I never got past the German Shepherd. I did manage to get their attention, however. Unfortunately, they know about this place. Kate may have told them. Last week, I got a death threat taped to the gate. I've had to change my cell number because they found it and started calling me up at all hours."

"What do you know about this guy she's with?" Lilly asked.

"Not a lot. His name is Leroy Burns. A white trash piece of scum if there ever was one," she said, sounding like the privileged Southern belle she might have once been. "He's mid-twenties and must be some kind of Pied Piper with the ladies. Kate met him in Narcotics Anonymous, not that I necessarily believe that. Kate isn't into any white supremacy bullshit or is even remotely political. The only reason I can see why she's with him is rebellion. That and she likes the bad boys. He's cat nip."

"Is there any chance she's being kept there against her will?"

Ranier shrugged. "I don't know. She hasn't called me in over three weeks, and she doesn't answer when I call. Look, I just don't want to see her get caught up in something. I'm worried the asshole boyfriend will hold up a liquor store and she'll be along for the ride. Something goes wrong and suddenly she becomes an accomplice."

"I have to ask," Soledad said. "Say we get her back here. Then what? You really think she'll stay? Or worse yet, if they know where she is, what's to keep them from coming here and…"

"Take her back? Kill me? Look, I'm not afraid of them. I just don't have the means to get her out of there. That's why I called Jeronimo."

Lilly really wanted to ask her why she thought Jeronimo would grant her such a favor, but decided now wasn't the time.

"Okay," Soledad said. "Give us the address and we'll check it out."

Hattie ripped a piece of paper from a notepad and jotted something down before handing it to him.

"We'll be in touch," Lilly said, getting to her feet. "By the way, do you have a photo of her?"

Ranier again seemed to hesitate. "No, nothing recent."

"Can you at least describe her?"

She sighed. "She's five foot six, a hundred and ten pounds, hazel eyes, dirty blonde hair and has a tattoo of the rising sun on her back. At least that's the only one I've ever seen. She's a pretty girl."

"How about a last name?" Lilly asked.

"It's Warden. Kate Warden."

"A date of birth?"

"I don't understand why you need to know that." "Okay," she said when her rejoinder was met with silence. "February 27th, 2005."

"Thanks. We'll be in touch."

"Please do," Ranier said to their backs as they walked out.

Neither of them said anything until they were back in the car. "I still think this is a shit show without a happy ending," Lilly said.

Soledad nodded but didn't say anything. They passed through the gate and turned onto the road leading aback to the interstate. Soledad slowed as they approached the van parked beside the road. This time, he stopped abreast of it and stared at the man sitting behind the wheel.

Lilly could just make out that the man was bearded, had long black hair tied back in ponytail, and had several earrings. The man turned and stared back at Soledad before turning away and saying something to another man sitting in the passenger seat who was difficult to make out. Soledad studied them for another few more seconds and drove off.

"Are you thinking what I'm thinking?" Lilly asked.

"I can't say for sure, but we might want to warn Punna not to leave the house unless she's carrying something besides her prayer beads and her attitude. Something about all this just doesn't seem right. Lots of loose ends."

"Yeah," was all she could come up with. The whole set up, Jeronimo's caginess, the Ranier woman's own seeming evasiveness, and then there was the girl herself. That was what bothered her the most. It raised flags for her in a way that elicited too many memories.

"What are you thinking?"

"I think I'm hungry."

"Let's grab some lunch and get settled in," Soledad said. "Then I'm going back to the airport and trade in this rental for something they haven't seen us in yet."

"Okay. But give me the address and I'll check it out on Google maps."

"Sounds like a plan," Soledad said, all the while watching in the rear-view mirror. "And let the shit show begin."

After lunch at a Denny's, they checked into their rooms at The Westin. Soledad left Lilly so he could return to the airport and exchange their car. Lilly said she would text Jeronimo and inform him they had arrived and had met with Hattie Ranier. She also intended to call Ranier and tell her about the van parked outside of her gate.

On the way to the car rental, Soledad noticed a U-Haul office. He turned in the car and then took a cab back to the U-Haul and rented a small van. He figured if there was any possibility that they might have to abduct Kate a van would prove a more suitable vehicle.

On the drive back to the hotel, he considered their options. The least attractive seemed to be a frontal assault on the house and removing Kate by force. The better choice would be if they could somehow isolate her and avoid any direct confrontation with her boyfriend or his fellow gang members.

At the very least, they would need firearms. It was easy enough to buy a handgun in Texas. There wasn't even a waiting period. You merely had to fill out some paperwork for an ATF background check. The problem was he no longer possessed a Texas driver's license. His US passport listed a Florida address. When he last renewed it, he wanted to avoid any Texas connection. So he flew to Miami, rented an apartment, and applied for a Florida driver's license.

It meant they would have to make an off the books purchase. There were most likely plenty of stolen handguns for the asking. If something happened where they needed to use one, it might be better anyway to have something that couldn't be traced back to them. This also meant finding a supplier, an option fraught with its own downsides. There was always the option of purchasing something at a gun show, but the time element might make that impractical.

He stopped for a cup of coffee at Starbucks and pulled out the contact number Jeronimo had provided him. The person answered on the first ring.

"*Si, quién es?*" the voice on the other end asked.

"*Un amigo de Jeronimo.*"

"No shit. How is the old goat?"

"He still has his horns. He said you could help me with some things."

"Such as?'

"I need hardware. The kind I can't get at Home Depot."

There was a pause at the other end. "I gotta tell you I'm out of town, otherwise it would be easy enough. I can give you another number to try."

"Is this person reliable?"

The man laughed. "Reliable? Mebbe. Trustworthy? He's no fucking Boy Scout, but that's what you get when you shop on the street. Just tell him Sancho referred you."

Soledad called the number Sancho had given him, and it rang for at least ten rings before anyone answered.

"You know what you want. Tell me, mon." The guy sounded Jamaican.

"Sancho said you could help me. I need a couple of… pieces."

"You mean glizzys? You not five 0?"

"What? The ops call you and place phone orders?"

"No, mon. I careful is all. Clizzys. Matics, Glocks you want?"

"Two of them. I need them tonight."

The guy made a whistling sound. "I can do. Here my address. Eight o'clock. No be late."

"How much?"

"One gran."

Soledad jotted down the address and hung up. He had one more stop to make. He found a Dollar Store and bought a roll of Duct tape. To his surprise, he also found a rack of pepper spray prominently displayed behind the checkout register. Thus equipped, he headed back to the hotel.

Lilly answered her door dressed in what appeared to be the same gym outfit she had worn the evening before at Jeronimo's. After filling her in on what he had accomplished, she did the same. She pulled up the Google map that showed the neighborhood where the house was located. It stood on a side street a couple of blocks from a four lane highway. There appeared to be a commercial strip of retail establishments on the street just behind the house. A closer view showed a rundown, two-story house, the bare yard enclosed by a cyclone fence.

"The highway nearby is good if we need to get out fast," she said. "There's something else. I tried to find something on Kate Warden. Arrest or court records, birth certificate, anything, but came up empty. It's probably because all her records are sealed because she was a minor. Otherwise, nothing. Do you think Ranier's telling us everything?"

"You think she'd lie? Come on. She's a nun for God's sake," he said with obvious sarcasm. "It wouldn't surprise me. The question is why."

"I did find stuff on the boyfriend. He's got a rap sheet a foot long. Drug possession, assault, possession of a stolen firearm, and so forth. He's done a couple of stints in county lockup but never hard time. They've had trouble making a case on some of the more serious charges."

"Mug shots?"

She opened her laptop and turned it so he could see. There were several mug shots taken at different times. The first one showed a Hollywood handsome man with curly black hair and cocksure smile. Another showed him appearing more disheveled as if he were high or intoxicated. The third showed the same handsome countenance if one discounted the shaved head and a tattoo of some sort snaking up his neck. He did still, however, have the same smug grin.

"Let's take a drive and check out the house before it gets dark."

It had started to rain, a light drizzle that shrouded everything in a gray film. That and the rush hour traffic meant it took an hour to find the neighborhood. The address revealed a shabby two-story house they had seen on Google Maps. A pair of late model, tricked out pickup trucks sat parked on the crumbling sidewalk. Inside the yard sat another truck that was in the process of being cannibalized for parts. A German Shepherd tethered to a chain paced back and forth in front of the porch.

"Seems like a nice enough place," Lilly remarked. "What do we do about the dog?"

"I've got some pepper spray."

"I tried that once. It must be like cat nip for pit bulls." She flashed on the memory of her fleeing for her life and empty-handed out of a liquor store in Dearborn.

They drove around the block one more time, noting parking spots and areas of concealment before calling it a day and returning to the hotel. They had missed happy hour. Soledad waited as Lilly changed into jeans and a sweater and they went downstairs to the bar.

They each had a margarita and shared an order of calamari, killing time until they needed to meet their gun dealer. The address was somewhere in a suburb called Baytown on the south side of the city. Neither of them had much to say, each lost in thought regarding what the next day or two might bring.

"I don't like this. Not one bit," Lilly said, breaking the silence.

"So you've said at least a half-dozen times."

"Jeronimo knew all along this wasn't going to be as simple as he made it sound. Doesn't it bother you that what we're probably doing is bordering on criminal?"

"Are you forgetting that's what we are? Criminals. Black hearts," he said with a grin. "My old man called anyone who might be a little bent a black heart. It made no difference if they were murders or shoplifters. Black hearts one and all."

"I don't see my heart as black. It's more like gray. A sort of light shade of gray." She had long ago concluded that there were no lighter shades of black.

"Look, think of it this way. We're just returning a parole jumper."

"That's easy for you to say. Say we get busted. I don't care what Jeronimo told me about my record being wiped clean. But my prints are going to be in the system. Sure, I've got a Mexican passport and new name. That'll make them come down on me even harder."

Soledad didn't know what to tell her. Hopefully, the cops would never get involved. Or so he hoped. He looked at his watch.

"We should go. This guy wants a grand. Do you have that on you?"

"Sure."

"This place is on the other side of town. Out past Pasadena near the ship channel. A place called Baytown. What? You know it?" he asked, reading her look of dismay.

"Not really," she replied, finishing her drink. What was she going to say? That she knew a couple of cheap motels and a few bars near there?

He finished his drink and motioned for the check. "Let's roll."

Even at this time of the night, the traffic was far from light. They slipped into the throat of downtown Houston and through the gleaming corridors of high rise office buildings before heading south toward Galveston. Most of what Lilly recalled about Houston's south side was the endless web of interconnecting freeways, the cancerous sprawl of shopping malls, car dealerships, strip joints, and retail stores of every imaginable stripe. The lack of any kind of obvious zoning restrictions also resulted in land-locked pockets of residential neighborhoods and apartment buildings. They passed several exits for Pasadena and finally took the one leading to Deer Park and Baytown.

Soon they spotted the sprawl of the towers of the refineries that were lit up like Christmas trees. The candle-like chimneys of gas flare gave an orange glow to the low hanging clouds. As they crossed over a long causeway spanning the Houston Ship Channel, Soledad opened his phone and passed it to Lilly.

"You navigate. I already entered the address on the GPS."

The directions led them through several miles of what looked to be middle class residential neighborhoods that eventually gave way to rows of low-slung apartment buildings. Lilly directed them through several narrow streets that eventually led to a dead end at a pocket of modest tract houses. She read off the street number, but it took a couple of passes before they found the correct mailbox. Soledad took back his phone and punched in a number.

"We're here," he said simply and waited for a short response before opening his door.

"Hold on," she said. "Are you sure about this? I mean about that we might need guns."

"Are you serious? Look, I'd rather err on the side of caution. Who knows? Maybe we won't need them."

"And this is our only option? Tomorrow is Friday, right? There's bound to be a gun show somewhere on Saturday. I bet we can buy something there no questions asked."

"We're here. I say let's do it."

"Okay," she said, still unconvinced. "But hang on." She opened her bag and took out the envelope with the cash Jeronimo had given her. She counted out a thousand and stuck it back in her bag. She placed the rest of the cash back in the envelope and stuffed it beneath the seat.

"One more thing. Give me some of that pepper spray. I like to err on the side of caution, too."

He shrugged and leaned over and opened the glove box. "Just be careful where you aim it," he said, handing her one of the canisters

The humid night air carried the funky smell of the ship channel overlaid with the almost sickly sweet and sulfurous stench of the nearby refineries. They made their way up a cracked, uneven sidewalk littered with rolls of neglected newspapers and a couple of overturned tricycles. A single bare light bulb illuminated a small porch stacked with cardboard boxes.

Soledad had no sooner knocked before the door was flung open revealing a petite, young black woman dressed in a shiny, tight-fitting miniskirt and a T-shirt that did little to conceal her bountiful breasts. She nodded with her head for them to follow her and started off down a darkened hallway.

They passed a couple of closed doors, behind one of which Lilly could hear a television broadcasting what sounded like a cartoon. The woman led them to a brightly lit, large, and a surprisingly modern kitchen equipped with the kind of immense, stainless-steel refrigerators and stoves one might find in a commercial kitchen. Suspended above the oven ranges were what looked like industrial grade venting hoods. Lilly guessed the occupants weren't caterers.

In the middle of what might have been the dining room, a massively obese black man of indeterminate age sat on a cracked leather sofa that had seen better days. He had dreadlocks and a long beard that reached to his knees. He wore cut-off denims, an Aloha shirt that barely managed to cover his girth, and one of those multi-colored, striped Rasta tams perched precariously atop his expansive tresses.

It took a moment before Lilly noticed another man standing casually in the corner. He was a tall, lean white guy with an acne-scarred face and attired in black biker leathers. The big man on the sofa studied them for a long moment before smiling.

"You are Jaime? Who dis goodie?" he said, nodding at Lilly. "She godas, mon."

Soledad looked around the kitchen before settling his gaze on the man standing in the corner. "You have what we talked about?" he said, turning back to the man on the sofa.

"Yah, mon. Say to me. Tell me how I know you not five oh?"

"If I was five oh, do you think I'd show up here to buy two fucking guns? Come on, man."

Lilly could tell something in Soledad's body language that indicated he was on edge, as if maybe he sensed something didn't seem right.

"Why you not sit? You like a drink? Captain Morgan? Mebbe one small toke?" he asked, hoisting a large bong and looking at each of them in turn.

"No thanks," Soledad said.

The man nodded. "Precious," he said, turning to the woman who had settled in a barstool at the end of the counter. "Dis big man ting. Yu go wait wit the pickneys."

The young woman offered a smirk and disappeared down the hallway. They heard a door open and then slam.

"I don' like ooman in my business," he said, smiling at Lilly with a mouthful of gold teeth. "But yu, godas. Yu look like some kine busyness ooman."

Lilly offered a smile and then glanced at the man in the corner.

"Look," Soledad said. "We're sort of in a hurry."

The Jamaican nodded and with great effort struggled to his feet. He lumbered over to a closet, its door secured with a trio of heavy door locks. He unlocked the first two with a set of keys attached to his immense waist by a thin cable. The third lock required him to enter a punch code. He opened the door and reached in and brought out a large plastic shopping bag. He set it on to a nearby counter and opened it.

"Yu aks for matics. Glocks," he said, gesturing for Soledad to come and inspect them.

Soledad glanced at the other man who had casually moved behind Lilly. Soledad reached into the bag and retrieved one of the Glocks. He checked the action before placing it back in the bag before checking out the other gun.

"We'll take them. We need a couple of extra magazines and ammo if you have it."

"No problem, mon," he replied and reached back into the closet and brought out a small cardboard box.

Soledad took a moment to examine the contents before setting it back on the counter. "You said a thousand."

No, mon, One gran dolla each."

'That's not what you said. A thousand each seems a bit steep. One thousand or we go somewhere else."

The fat man stared at Soledad for a moment and then smiled. "Wah di rass? Mebbe one gran and five hundred moah."

"No. One thousand. That's all the cash we brought."

The Jamaican's smile turned scornful. "Mebbe we take gran and let yu go. But no matics."

Soledad looked at Lilly with what seemed almost comic dismay.

"Look," Lilly said. "I'll show you what we have. Then we make a deal," she said, reaching into her bag, turning to glance at the biker guy standing behind her. He leaned in closer to watch her begin to rummage in her bag.

"Shit. Hold this, would you?" she said, handing him her wallet and a set of keys. She let the wallet slip out of her hand and drop to the floor. As the biker bent down to pick it up, Lilly pulled the pepper spray from her bag, and as he straightened, she launched a long spray in the guy's face. He cursed and stumbled backwards, swiping at his face. As he struggled to regain his balance, he fumbled at something in his waistband.

"Gun!" Soledad shouted.

Lilly kicked the biker in the groin. As he bent over in pain, she kneed him in the face. The gun clattered to the floor.

"Shit," she yelled, grabbing her knee in pain. She looked at Soledad and the Jamaican who both appeared surprised by the sudden, unforeseen violence. Before the Jamaican could react, Soledad shoved him back against the closet door, causing the Jamaican to lose his balance and slide down the wall. He tried to right himself, but his bulk only allowed him to get to his knees.

Lilly scooped up the biker's gun from the floor and walked over to the Jamaican. "You asshole," she said, pressing the barrel against his forehead and pulling back the hammer of the revolver.

"Lilly," Soledad said calmly. "Leave it. Let's go. Come on. Lilly," he said again when she made no effort to pull back.

"Lilly! Goddammit! Let's go."

She hesitated for several seconds before finally lowering the gun and smiling at the Jamaican. "Your lucky day, shit bag."

Soledad snatched up the bag of guns and the cardboard box, and then paused just long enough to slam home a magazine into one of the Glocks. Lilly scooped up her wallet and keys from the floor.

"We keep this as a bonus," she said, waving the revolver in front of the Jamaican's face before limping down the hallway.

"Are you okay?" Soledad asked, catching up to her.

"Let's just get the hell out of here."

One of the doors opened, and the young black woman appeared in the doorway. Soledad raised the Glock and she quickly shut the door.

"Watch our backs," he said as they piled into the car. He punched the starter button, slammed the car into reverse and accelerated down the narrow street. They were halfway down the block before the Jamaican lumbered out onto the porch, clutching what looked to be a rifle or a shotgun. He managed to get off a couple of rounds, but nothing found its mark.

Neither of them said anything until they started over the causeway. She leaned over to glance at the clock on the dash. "Goodie. We still have time for a drink."

Soledad pulled his eyes away from the evening news on the television above the bar and glanced at Lilly. She seemed distracted ever since they arrived back at the hotel. They hadn't exchanged more than a handful of words on the entire drive back. He had no idea what she was thinking, and for some reason was reluctant to ask.

As for him, he kept replaying in his mind what had gone wrong with what should have been a simple transaction. He worried that the fiasco might result in blowback directed at Sancho, Jeronimo's Houston contact. If so, he was certain they would eventually hear about it.

He also couldn't help but think about how Lilly had dealt with the situation. Jeronimo was right in telling him not to underestimate her. He could also see why Jeronimo had chosen her, for she had shown herself to be a lot more than a simple courier. He thought about what Jeronimo had revealed to him about Lilly's past. It made him wonder how much Jeronimo didn't know about her, or possibly was reluctant to divulge.

Her response to the debacle at the Jamaican's convinced him that Lilly could think on her feet and was fearless. That or she was foolhardy, or simply crazy. Whatever she was, he felt confident that one of these attributes would either come in handy or screw things up.

"You weren't really going to shoot him, were you?" he asked.

She looked at him with what soldiers called a thousand yard stare. Her thoughts were obviously somewhere far removed from the Westin bar or the house in Baytown.

She shrugged and gave him a dead pan look. "I don't know. Probably not."

"Probably not?" He rattled the ice in his glass and tipped it back. "Maybe one more," he said, motioning to the bartender. "I was thinking we should get up early and set up surveillance at the house. We need to see who comes and goes. If it looks like the boyfriend leaves, we might risk going in. I just don't want to resort to gunplay. No one needs to get hurt. You agree?"

She didn't reply and still seemed distracted.

"Lilly. Are you okay?"

"I was just thinking. Has Jeronimo ever seemed to you to be the sentimental type?"

"You're still questioning his motive?'

"Aren't you? I mean all this for some woman who jilted him a long time ago. You know him better than I do," she said after taking a swallow of her margarita. "How long have you been with him? I heard six or seven years."

"Coming up on seven."

"If you don't mind me asking, how did you end up working for him?"

He let his reply hang there a long while as he edited what he should and shouldn't divulge to her. In the end, he decided she deserved to know. What would it hurt? He downed what remained of his drink and turned in his seat to face her.

"After I got my walking papers in San Antonio, I drifted around. I had couple of dead end jobs. It wasn't like I had a glowing job reference. I finally got a gig down in Brownsville babysitting this wealthy rancher's daughter. She was a co-ed at the local community college. A spoiled, over ripe piece of work that might as well had the word caution tattooed on her forehead in big red letters. Needless to say, it didn't work out. Then one day I get a call from a guy I used to hang with in San Antonio. It happened to be the same asshole that got me involved in the fiasco that got me fired. He got screwed in the same deal so I never held it against him.

"Anyway, we get to talking and he says he wants to make it up to me with an easy, guaranteed one night job that would pay a thousand. I should've known right away then that nothing's that easy, but I was broke. He said he'd done this same job once before without a hitch. It was simple as driving stolen cars across the border into Mexico. Easy money and never any hassles, he said."

"I've heard that line before," she said. "More than once."

He nodded. "We were supposed to pick up the cars in McAllen and drive them across the border at Reynosa to a ranch outside of Monterrey. The customs agents on both sides were paid off. And if we were ever asked, we'd have bogus registration papers. There were three of us that night. Me, my so-called friend, and this young kid from Dallas. We were all driving these brand new Expeditions that we picked up at this warehouse in McAllen. The Mexican who handed us the keys told us we'd be shuttled back by morning. He had us leave a half hour apart to make us look less conspicuous at the border. I was the last one to leave."

Soledad paused as the bartender brought their drinks before going on.

"The guy gave us these cards we were supposed to show to the customs agents at the border. The agent on our side didn't even bother to look. He just waved me through. The Mexican agent at least looked at the card."

"I'm curious. What was on the card?" Lilly asked.

"Just this red star and what might have been a phone number. So I head south and it occurs to me that maybe we're transporting something else besides the Expedition we're driving. But what? I'm going into Mexico for God's sake. It couldn't be drugs. That didn't make any sense."

Lilly started to say something, but then thought twice and merely shook her head.

"So I crossed the border at one in the morning and was told to show up at this ranch fifty clicks north of Monterrey at one-thirty. No sooner, no later. The place was easy enough to find. Rancho Opuntia. It had this big sign you couldn't miss. So I turn onto this dirt road and I drive a couple of miles in, and I see what I think are headlights up ahead."

He paused to have a swallow of his drink and think about the order of the things that happened next. "I knew it was all fucked up as soon as I drove up on them."

RANCHO OPUNTIA
NUEVO LEON, MEXICO

2017

Soledad slowed and leaned over the steering wheel to make out what he was seeing. It was a clearing of some sort. He could just make out what might have been a wooden corral. Parked beside it were a half-dozen vehicles, all with their headlights on and grouped together in a sort of semi-circle. He immediately recognized the two other SUVs. There were also three or four pickups and what looked to be a Mercedes sedan parked off to the side.

Out of caution, he came to a stop twenty yards from the vehicles. Three men carrying automatic rifles stepped into the circle cast by the headlights and began walking towards him.

He carefully slipped the SUV into reverse, but before he could do anything, he saw the headlights of another vehicle come up close behind him, blocking any retreat. It was only then he saw bodies sprawled in the dirt in front of the phalanx of parked vehicles. From what he could tell, there appeared to be six bodies. In that instant, he recognized the red wind breaker on one of the bodies. He remembered the kid from

Dallas had been wearing it. Then he noticed a man kneeling off to the side with his hands behind his head.

"Shit, shit, shit," he muttered. What had he stumbled into? He reached for the door handle. Part of him told him to run, but he knew his chances of escaping were nonexistent. Instead, he froze. For a long moment, nothing seemed to happen. The three men with the rifles had stopped and stood staring at him.

Suddenly, a tall man dressed in a dark suit and tie emerged from between the gunmen and began walking towards him. Soledad could see he carried what appeared to be a hand gun in his right hand. The man stopped ten feet from Soledad's vehicle and motioned with his free hand for Soledad to get out of the SUV and come forward.

Realizing he had little choice, Soledad dismounted and walked up to the man. It was difficult to make out the man's face in the back lit glare of the headlights. The man studied Soledad for a moment before turning to glance back at the bodies sprawled in the dirt behind him.

"Your friends," he said, turning back to Soledad. "The wrong place at the wrong time."

He spoke softly and with only the slightest of any accent. He nodded in the direction of the two Expeditions. All of their doors including the rear hatches stood open. The rear seats had been pulled out and dumped to the side. A handful of crates and some black garbage bags lay off to the side.

"You are American?" the man asked.

Soledad's mouth was so dry that it took a moment to answer.

"Yeah." He licked his lips and swallowed back the bile rising in his throat. "Look, I was just hired to deliver the SUV. I don't know anything about..."

"I know that," the man said, cutting him off. He turned and pointed with his gun at the man kneeling beside the bodies. "This man is responsible for the death of your friends. It is only right that you should be allowed to exact your revenge," he said, holding out the gun to Soledad. When Soledad made no effort to take it, the man grabbed Soledad's wrist and pressed the gun into his hand.

"Wait. You want me to kill that guy?"

"*Si.* It is your right."

Soledad wondered if the man was merely toying with him. It might just be some kind of cruel trick. Out of some misguided instinct, Soledad worked the automatic's action and ejected a round. One of the men with an automatic rifle stepped up behind the man in the suit and pointed his rifle at Soledad. For a second, Soledad thought he might be able to shoot his way out of this before deciding it would prove to be suicidal.

"No," he said, holding out the gun to the man.

"*¿Por qué?* He and his men killed your friends."

"I don't shoot unarmed men."

The man considered Soledad for a long moment before clicking his tongue and taking the gun. He turned to the man with the rifle standing behind him.

"*Llévalo a mi auto,*" he said and started to walk away.

"*Esperar,*" Soledad said. "*Yo no lo hice…*I didn't have anything to do with this."

The man turned and looked at him. "*¿Tú hablas Español?*"

Soledad nodded. "*Si.*"

The man considered this for a moment "*Muy bien.* Wait for me at the car. I will give you a ride."

The man with the rifle gestured with his head for Soledad to follow him. He led him to the Mercedes and opened the passenger side door. Soledad crawled in and the door slammed shut behind him.

He sat there staring into the darkness and tried to make out what was happening. He had obviously stumbled onto something that had gone horribly wrong, but what exactly? He reached over to see if there were keys in the ignition, but there was no such luck. It would be foolhardy to try to escape anyway.

A minute or so passed before he heard a single gunshot. He turned to look over his shoulder, but the line of pickups blocked his view. Another minute or so passed before his door was flung open. It was the man in the suit.

"You will drive," he said, handing Soledad the keys.

Soledad got out and walked around the front of the car. He could now see that the men with the rifles were loading the bodies into the back of one of the trucks. He slid behind the wheel.

The man in the suit dropped heavily into the passenger seat and then opened the glove compartment and placed the handgun inside. Soledad could smell the cordite.

"Now, you will tell me how you came to be here," the man said.

"He shot him?" she asked. "Jeronimo shot the guy?"

A pained look fell across Soledad's face as he met her look. "I don't know."

"What do you mean you don't know?"

"I mean, I want to think he didn't. He never said. For all I know he might've had one of his men shoot the guy. What do you think? Do you think he's capable of that?"

She didn't answer. Part of her told her that she was surely not one to judge. She had done as much. Did it really surprise her that Jeronimo could execute someone in cold blood? On the one hand, she knew Jeronimo to be a pragmatist. And she also recognized him to be a man of contradictions, especially when it came to any moral codes or boundaries. But was Jeronimo what Soledad had referred to as a black heart? If he was, then what did that say about the color of her soul? In the end, all she knew was that Soledad's story would no doubt color her view of Jeronimo.

She started to raise her glass of tequila to her mouth, but then realized her hands were shaking. This unrealized side of Jeronimo aside, Soledad's account had stirred up her usual angst. Part of it was still the white hot surge of anger she had felt when she pointed the gun at the Jamaican. It was also the realization of just how close she had come to acting on that irrational rage. She had acted on that same reckless impulse more than once before. And she remembered both the satisfaction and yes, the shame she had experienced. At times, the memory overpowered her, buried her, defying the weight of any words to describe what she felt. .

"Are you okay?"

"I'm fine," she replied, gripping her glass with both hands. "So what was that all about?" she asked. "I mean, what went down out there on that ranch?"

"Obviously someone fucked up. It turns out that the guy kneeling there was one of Jeronimo's right hand men. It seemed the guy tried to strike out on his own and was smuggling guns in for Los Zetas. He was also dealing in Mexican black tar and using the SUVs to bring back cash that he'd been laundering stateside."

"And Jeronimo found out?"

Soledad nodded. "And decided he had to nip it in the bud. Make an example of the guy. Jeronimo and his men got there too late to save my friend and the other driver. I lucked out in getting there after it had all gone down. You know Jeronimo's not a smuggler, and he sure as hell doesn't tolerate any drug dealing. Right hand man or not, the guy had to go. You asked if Jeronimo's the sentimental type. I guess not."

"So, what about afterward. In the car?"

"I ended up driving him back to Mexico City. And we talked. At first, he just wanted to talk about superficial stuff. Food. Football. I'm sorry to say he's a Cowboy's fan," he said with a smirk. "Then he told me about the guy he had just shot. He'd been working for Jeronimo for almost ten years. Jeronimo had even been the best man at the guy's wedding. If you want to know if I thought Jeronimo was sorry about it. Sure. You could tell he was disappointed, pissed off, and yeah, he was sorry about it. But..." Soledad shrugged. "I guess it was just business. Just the nature of the game."

They both fell silent for a moment. She finished off her tequila and looked at him.

"I must be delusional to think I got out of that world. I've been telling myself that Jeronimo's just a businessman who bends the rules a bit. That I'm just his delivery girl."

"He's not like the rest of them. Not like those cartel assholes. You have to know that."

She shrugged. "I want to believe it. So you still haven't told me why he hired you," she said, hoping to change the subject.

"I told him I used to be a cop. The next thing I know he offers me a job. He said that after what just went down, he needed an extra set of eyes. I told him I wouldn't shoot anyone in the back of the head. Or be driving any cars across the border. He seemed alright with that. And here I am. End of story."

"Why did you tell me all this?"

"Because you asked. Remember?" He looked at her in a way that telegraphed hesitation. "You should know that I've never told anyone that story. I thought you of all people would understand."

"Understand? What? Understand what?"

"I don't know. I thought we were alike."

"We're not anything alike," she replied with a flare of anger. "I don't know what Jeronimo told you, but you don't know me. You think because… Look, I'm not denying I've been in and out of trouble with the law since I threw away my last Barbie doll. I've been in prison twice. I've…"

Killed people, she almost blurted out.

"But just because we both work for Jeronimo doesn't mean we're alike. Okay?"

"I'm sorry. I didn't mean anything," he said. "I just thought…" He rattled the ice in his glass and looked at her. "What was it like? Prison, I mean?"

"You're really starting to piss me off. You know that?" She stared at her glass for a long moment before saying anything. "Female rot," she muttered softly. Wasn't that how she had described it to Harlan that morning in the diner in Las Cruces after her so-called escape from Perryville Prison?

"Twenty-four seven having to share your life with pissed off people. You don't what that's like. It crushes you." She took a sip of her tequila. "All these women with fucked up lives because of bad choices, bad luck. Yeah, female rot. Who knows? Maybe it's the same for men. Wasting away your best years. But it's different for women, I think." She turned and looked at him. "Look, Soledad..."

"It Jaime," he said.

"I don't mean to be a bitch. It's just… the shit that went down with the Jamaican, and then you telling me that story. I guess it just touched a nerve."

He nodded and looked at his watch. "I'm turning in."

"I think I'll stay and have another drink."

"Okay. I'll knock on your door at six-thirty and we'll check out the house. See you," he said and walked off.

She hoisted her empty glass at the bartender. Another drink would help her fall asleep, not that she would stay asleep. Like always, she would undoubtedly awaken in the middle of the night in a cold sweat, the memory of her abduction and captivity at that ranch back in Sonora swirling into her consciousness. And as always, dawn would find her curled into a fetal position and drenched in sweat.

She nodded her gratitude to the bartender as he topped off her glass and promptly downed half of it, knowing tonight would prove to be no different.'

She startled at the sound of her cell phone chirping. As she fumbled to find it, she knocked her laptop off the night stand. She cursed and switched on the bedside lamp. The clock on the night stand read 5:18AM. She picked up the phone and squinted at the number, and even in her state of semi-consciousness, she knew who was calling.

"Hello," she whispered hoarsely.

There was silence for a moment before Hattie Ranier asked, "Lilly, right?"

"Speaking."

"I'm sorry for waking you up."

"It's okay. I wasn't really asleep. Why are you calling?"

"Something's happened. Can you come here?"

"Yeah, I guess so. Can you tell me what this is about?" she asked, falling back on her pillow

"You'll see when you get here. And leave your sidekick behind," she said and disconnected.

She sat up, swung her legs over the side, and paused, wondering why Ranier didn't want Soledad to come along. Part of her thought that Ranier was going to reveal things she was hesitant to do so the day before in Soledad's presence. Or maybe she just had a problem with men. She slipped on a pair of jeans and a sweatshirt, peed, brushed her teeth, and was out the door. She knocked several times on Soledad's door before he opened it wearing only a pair of boxers.

"Don't get any ideas," she said in response to his look of puzzlement. "I need the car keys. Ranier called and she wants me to come there," she explained before he could get a word out. "She said something's happened."

"Did she say what?"

"No, just that I'd see when I got there."

"Let me get dressed," he said, turning away.

"She said I should come without you."

He turned back and looked at her.

"Woman business maybe," she said. "Give me the keys."

He considered her a moment and then turned and went over to a dresser and returned with the keys.

"You're sure about this?"

"My intuition tells me she wants to spill her guts."

"Call me. I'll take an Uber to the house and keep watch. And be careful. They may still be watching her house."

It was raining heavily when she slipped out of the hotel's parking garage, but by the time she reached the road to the Refuge it had slowed to a light drizzle. As she drew near, she passed a fire truck heading in the opposite direction. She slowed at the gate leading to Ranier's property, but had to stop to allow a Harris County Sheriff's Department cruiser to pull out. Something had undoubtedly happened.

The first thing she saw when she reached the house was the smoldering, skeletal frames of two vehicles parked in the graveled lot. Hattie Ranier stood on the porch. She wore a bright yellow rain slicker over what appeared to be pajamas. Lilly pulled up in front of the porch and got out. She studied the smoldering wrecks for a moment before joining Ranier on the porch.

"What happened?"

"What does it look like? They didn't have to burn my housekeeper's car, too. Those asshole fuckers. They…"

She caught herself, closed her eyes and took a couple of slow, deep breaths. "I'm sorry," she said with a faint smile. "I should practice what I preach. Acceptance. And *anichcha*. You know what that means? Impermanence." She sighed. "It's just a damn car."

Lilly nodded. "It makes me wonder though if some asshole had torched the Buddha's oxcart, if the Enlightened One might've called the guy an asshole. Under his breath, of course. And you're sure it was them?"

"Of course it was. The sheriff's deputy said someone spray painted over the lens of my security camera so there's no hard evidence. But it was them."

"Did you tell the cops about the van we saw?"

"I described it to them and gave them the address where they could probably find it."

"I suspect they'll roust them," Lilly said. "And if they do, they're likely scoop up Kate. Maybe send her back here. That may change things. Or not."

Ranier didn't say anything, but simply stood there with her arms crossed.

"Are you sure you don't have any coffee?" Lilly asked.

"I've got some instant in my desk," Ranier confessed, her gaze still focused on the burned out vehicles. She turned abruptly and walked back inside. Lilly followed her.

The stench of smoke carried in to the house though Lilly detected what she thought might be the smell of something baking. Ranier asked her to wait in her office and disappeared down the hallway. Lilly took the opportunity to nose around her office.

She looked more closely at the photos on the wall. In the margin of the photo of the group of nuns was scrawled *Ordination Honolulu 2010*. The photo of the old woman in the rocker had no caption. Neither did the one of the young woman on the horse. Lilly leaned in closer and tried to make out the woman's face.

Maybe it was only her imagination, but the woman bore somewhat of a resemblance to Ranier. It was something about the jaw line, or the eyes. She wondered if the photo might be of Ranier when she was younger.

There wasn't much else in the office except for the chairs and a desk, its top clear of anything other than a couple of pens and a notepad. She opened the lone drawer an inch or two, but other than a box of paper clips and a Ziploc bag, it also appeared empty. She shut it just a few seconds before Ranier appeared in the doorway bearing a tray that held a teapot, two cups, and what looked to be a plate of muffins.

"You're in luck. One of the girls made fresh muffins."

She set the tray down on the desk and then opened the drawer and removed a Ziploc bag of what appeared to be instant coffee. She poured them each a cup of hot water and slid the baggie of coffee across the desk along with a spoon and a couple of packets of creamer and sugar.

"What I'd really like with this instead of a muffin is a cigarette," Ranier said. She pantomimed holding a cigarette between her fingers and taking a long, luxurious draw. "Oh yeah," she said with obvious satisfaction. "Did you ever smoke?"

"I did when I was in prison," Lilly replied, hoping her candor might be reciprocated.

Ranier merely smiled. She watched Lilly spoon in three heaping spoonful's of the instant coffee into her cup.

"I have to ask. Are you and Jeronimo…You know. Together? An item?"

Lilly shook her head and smiled. "God, no. He's old enough to be my father. No, I'm just his delivery girl."

Ranier nodded. "I'm guessing you're more than that. I must admit that I expected him to send a couple of young toughs. *Cholos.* Isn't that what they're called? I imagined they'd come and kick ass and take names. But you… you've got too much finesse for that. But you're tough, too. Something tells me you've been chewed up and spit out more than once. Stumbled a few times."

Lilly didn't take the bait. "It still might come to that. Kicking ass and taking names, I mean. But that's Soledad's job."

Ranier nodded.

"Tell me something," Lilly said, glancing at the photo of the woman on the horse. "Is that you?"

"No. My daughter." A look of affliction, quick as a cat's paw, crossed her face and was just as quickly replaced with what might have been pleasure. "Bridget was her name." Ranier turned and looked at the photo.

"She died ten years ago next month. Suicide. The coroner said it was an accidental drug overdose as if that was any comfort." She turned and looked back at Lilly. "I raised her on my own. I wasn't really equipped for that. And I fucked it up. I got into Buddhism hoping it might help. If not her, then me."

She sighed deeply and looked away. "Buddha said one must be honest with oneself. And with others. Discard one's self-deception. *Sacca.* Truthfulness." She looked back at Lilly. "Kate's my granddaughter."

"I guessed as much. Or least I guessed she wasn't just some runaway."

"How?"

"When you gave us her birthdate without looking it up."

Ranier nodded. "So, you understand now. Kate was just eight when her mother died. As you might expect, she took it hard. Her father was no better equipped to be a parent than I was. He dropped out of the picture five years ago. Kate became my responsibility, which was her misfortune. She would came in and out of here, spent a year in a foster home. When she was sixteen she applied to be emancipated. Dropped out of school. After that, it was hard to keep tabs on her. She was for lack of a better word, feral. I've failed her. Just like I failed her mother."

Lilly looked away, the anguish of Ranier's confession scratching at her own wounds.

"There's one more thing I should tell you," Ranier said. "Her mother. Bridget. She was Jeronimo's daughter."

13

Lilly stared at her, unsure of her response. It made sense now. Or did it?

"You understand now?" Ranier asked.

"Yes. And no. He doesn't know?"

Ranier shook her head.

"And you never thought to tell him?"

"I suppose I was being selfish. And high-minded. It was the same reason I couldn't stay with Jeronimo. I couldn't abide what he was doing. I saw how he lived his life as being amoral. You must realize I spent four years in a convent school before I ran away from my parents. I may have been leading a less than a conventional lifestyle when Jeronimo and I met, but I was still the good Catholic girl in many ways. And I was afraid that if I told him about Bridget he would maybe take her from me. I wouldn't allow that."

"And you're sure he doesn't know?"

"How could he?"

"I guarantee he has ways." She thought of how he had found out about that her criminal records being expunged. It was beginning to all make sense of why he had deigned to help Ranier and allowed himself to become involved with a runaway with whom he had no obvious connection or investment in her wellbeing. The question is when did he know, and why hadn't he interceded before now.

"I think he knows. I mean didn't it ever occur to you that it was odd that he'd be so willing to help you? You call him out of the blue after what? Thirty something years? And he agrees to help?"

Ranier didn't say anything, but Lilly could tell from her expression that what Lilly had said made sense.

"Maybe it was my way of telling him," she said. "It might've been an unconscious decision on my part, that maybe I was giving him a chance. Does that make any sense? I needed him. After all this time, I needed him."

She looked at Lilly. "Are you going to tell him?"

"It's not my place to tell him."

Ranier didn't respond. This changes everything, Lilly thought. Soledad should know. The thought crossed her mind that he already knew. She glanced at her watch and realized she should've called him before now and told him about the cars being firebombed and that the police were likely going to the house to interrogate the gang members. Soledad would be there and could see if the cops took any of them in for further questioning, and if they did, whether Kate would be among them.

"I need to go. Soledad might be at the house. If the cops take her in, there's nothing we can do. I hope you have a good lawyer."

"I do. I'll call and give her a heads up."

"By the way, you said before you didn't have a photo of her, or at least a recent one."

Ranier opened a file box on the floor beneath the desk and pulled out a large manila envelope. "Here," she said, sliding it across the desk. "Since I don't seem to have any more secrets."

Lilly opened the envelope and withdrew a five by eight color photograph. It showed a smiling young woman with shoulder length dark brown hair. She had a broad mouth, high cheekbones, and hazel eyes. There was something challenging in the way she stared at the camera, defiance masking what Lilly recognized as vulnerability.

"She is pretty. This was taken in happier times?"

"Sixteenth birthday. The last time I saw her smile. Keep the photo if you think it will help. I just want her back safe."

"We'll do our best," Lilly said. She downed the rest of her coffee, grabbed a muffin and hurried out the door. She paused before getting into the U-Haul van and called Soledad.

14

By the time the Uber driver found the address, it began to rain heavily again. At least, Soledad had the presence of mind to buy an umbrella in the hotel gift shop. Unfortunately, the only color available was neon yellow. He had the driver circle the block hoping to find a spot that would provide a vantage point for watching the house. He was worried though he would be too conspicuous if he merely stood on the sidewalk holding a bright yellow umbrella.

On the second pass, Soledad spotted a house across the street and one house down. It displayed a For Rent sign posted in the yard. From the looks of the knee-high weeds in the yard and the overflowing mailbox, the house was unoccupied. Better yet, the front porch appeared shrouded in overgrown shrubbery. He would be able to watch the house without being observed.

As he paid the driver, he glanced over at the house. The van he and Lilly noticed the previous day parked on the road outside of the Zen Refuge now sat parked on the sidewalk. The two pickup trucks they had seen earlier were parked on the street in front.

He no sooner had settled in behind an overgrown oleander shrub when a police cruiser bearing the logo of the Harris County Sheriff's Department pulled up and stopped across the street and just down from the house. The two men inside made no effort to get out. As he watched them, his cell phone rang.

"Where are you?" Lilly asked before he could even answer.

"Watching the house. Where are you?"

"Just leaving Ranier's. They torched a couple of cars, and I think the cops may be on their way there to ask them about it."

"They're already here. A sheriff's unit just pulled up. Hang on," he said as he watched an unmarked Ford sedan pull up behind one of the pickup trucks. "Reinforcements just rolled up. You'd better get over here, but best keep it on the low down," he said and disconnected.

The two uniformed sheriff's officers crawled out of their cruiser and leaned against the fender. Soledad could see one of them was on the phone. Across the street, Soledad saw what he assumed were two plainclothes detectives emerging from the sedan. They hesitated a moment before walking up to the chain link gate.

A moment or two went by as the two detectives eyeballed the house. They had no doubt seen the German Shepherd chained up on the front porch. One of them began yelling something that Soledad couldn't catch. The dog began barking frantically. Several seconds went by before Soledad saw the front door of the house open. More yelling ensued; first from one of the detectives before being reciprocated by someone just inside the front door. One of the detectives opened the gate and stepped into the yard. The other one followed him and moved to a spot ten feet or so to the side of his partner. There was still yelling going on, mostly from inside the house, but it was impossible for Soledad to make out anything over the frenzied barking of the German Shepherd.

One of the sheriff's deputies reached inside the cruiser and pulled out what looked to be a shotgun. He walked cautiously into the middle of the street while his partner moved behind the cruiser.

It all went south in an instant. A burst of what sounded like automatic rifle fire shattered a front window of the house, cutting down the detective who had stepped to the side. The other detective drew his weapon as he dropped into a crouch and moved in the direction of the porch. Before he could make it another burst of fire this time from the open front door, cut him down, too.

Just then, two men ran out of the front door and sprinted for the van. The deputy in the street opened fire and dropped one of them, but the other returned fire with his automatic rifle. The brief firefight ended badly for the deputy for he staggered and fell wounded in the street.

The other deputy crouching behind the cruiser opened fire with his handgun but not in enough time to stop the van from taking off. Suddenly, a tall bearded man with a shaved head emerged from the front door carrying what appeared to be an AR-15. He raked a long volley at the sheriff's cruiser, the rounds thumping loudly against the side of the cruiser and shattering its windows.

Soledad saw the other deputy fall to the ground. He couldn't tell if he had been shot or was just attempting to take cover. Just then, another man dressed entirely in black charged out of the house. He was dragging a woman behind him by the arm. She was screaming and attempting to break free from his grip. She stumbled to the ground, and the man pulled her to her feet and shoved her into the pickup's cab. Soledad couldn't be sure, but the man resembled the mug shot they had seen of Leroy Burns.

The bearded guy leaned over the one fallen detective, seemed to say something, and then fired a burst into the detective's back. He then calmly walked out into the street towards the sheriff's cruiser. He paused at the fallen deputy, kicked him, and then picked up the deputy's shotgun.

Soledad saw the other deputy crawl to the cruiser's open passenger door and reach inside. Soledad still couldn't tell if the deputy had been shot. The assailant in the street started to walk casually towards the back of the cruiser.

Soledad pulled his Glock from his jacket, stepped off the porch, and started across the street. Somehow, the bearded guy didn't see Soledad until it was too late. Without thinking, as if acting out of some dormant instinct, Soledad put two rounds in the man's chest.

Soledad heard the pickup truck roaring off. For a second or two, Soledad considered letting off a few rounds, but instead walked over to the man he had just shot to make sure he was down. He saw it was the same man he and Lilly had seen sitting in the van on the road outside the Zen Refuge. He kicked the AR-15 and shotgun aside and then walked around to the other side of the cruiser. The deputy was trying to pull himself into the front seat while fumbling with the radio handset. Soledad leaned over and took it from him. The deputy, his face ashen and contorted in pain and terror, slumped back on the pavement. He looked absurdly young, a rookie perhaps. The deputy's hands were bloody, and now Soledad could see he was bleeding from a shoulder wound. Soledad could see where another round had fortunately struck the deputy's Kevlar vest.

Soledad clicked on the handset. "Officer down. Need immediate help. We're at..."

"I already know your position," the female voice on the radio said. "Help is on the way. Stand by."

"Assailant is fleeing the scene in a white Ford pickup with chrome wheels. Possibly heading towards Highway 290. Be advised he has a female hostage. Repeat, he has a female hostage. Copy?"

"Roger that."

Soledad could already hear sirens in the distance. With his shirttail he wiped the handset and dropped it on the seat.

"Hang in there," he said, looking down at the deputy. "You're going to make it."

Soledad turned and looked around. Down the block, a couple of young black men had hopped off a garbage truck and appeared to be cautiously approaching the scene. Soledad turned and began walking in the opposite direction when he remembered the umbrella. He hurried back to the porch to retrieve it. If someone had seen him come from the porch and told the police there was always the outside chance they would find the umbrella and check it for fingerprints.

The sirens were getting closer, so he began to walk down the block as quickly as he dared. When he reached the end of the block, he looked around to see if anyone was watching before wiping down the Glock with his shirttail and then tossing it into a storm drain. He set off again, this time more calmly.

A police cruiser slowed as it passed him and then sped by. Two ambulances followed. Soledad took out his phone. His hands were shaking so badly, he had difficulty dialing Lilly.

"A shit show just like you said. Don't go near the house. I'm on foot heading south on Mason Street I think. Hurry."

Soledad flagged down Lilly a block from a feeder road leading to Highway 290. She pulled over at the curb and Soledad crawled in.

"What happened? You had me worried. There're police cars all over the place."

"The skinheads reacted like shit heads. They killed three cops, wounded another one, and I'm pretty sure Burns took off with Kate."

"Holy shit!"

"It gets worse. I ended up shooting one of the skinheads."

"Wait. Back up and tell me from the beginning."

He began with the plainclothes detectives rolling up and how the confrontation had started to play out. He finished with him speaking to the dispatcher before walking away.

"People saw you, didn't they? Or at least the deputy did."

"I don't know who else might've seen it all. The wounded deputy for sure got a good look at me. Listen, we need to change hotels. Once this gets out on the news, my Uber driver might tell the cops about dropping off a blonde guy at the scene just before it went down. Once they hear that deputy's story, they'll be looking for me. If for no other reason than they ought to give me a fucking medal."

Neither of them had much to say for a minute or so. "It's over is all I can say," Lilly said, breaking the silence. "We did our part. Now let's go home."

"Turn here," he said, pointing to an alleyway behind a row of retail shops. "Stop at that last dumpster."

As soon as she stopped, he took off his sodden leather jacket and tossed it along with the umbrella into the dumpster.

Once back at the Westin, he let her go in first so she could pack up. He followed her upstairs five minutes later, quickly collected his things and went back down to the van.

While he waited for her to check out, he considered what might go wrong. The only problem he saw was if the Uber driver told the cops he had picked up his fare at the Westin and dropped him off across the street from the skinhead's place. He wasn't registered at the hotel as both rooms had been under Lilly's name. If the cops asked around, someone at the hotel might recall a man fitting his description. It would still be a long shot connecting him to Lilly. The only place they had been together had been the bar. Once Lilly had checked out of the room, it would prove to be a dead end. He figured that finding the anonymous bystander who had saved the deputy's life would be a low priority, at least at first.

The only other connection he could think of would be Ranier. The cops would most likely interrogate her again about why she had been targeted by the gang. He hoped she had enough presence of mind to be evasive and not bring up the fact she had arranged for someone to try and extract Kate. Again, any further questions regarding a link to the mystery bystander would hopefully end there.

A half hour later, they pulled up to a Holiday Inn Express near the interstate. To avoid any trail, Lilly booked a single room for one night and paid cash. Before going up to the room, they first stopped at a hair salon to buy some black hair dye, and then went to a sporting goods store where Soledad bought a Houston Astros shell jacket and a matching cap.

Back at the Holiday Inn, they walked separately up to their room. When Soledad walked in, he found Lilly sitting on the room's only bed.

"It's all they had," Lilly explained. "Don't get any ideas. You've already taken your life into your hands once today," she added with a grim smile.

Soledad dropped his bags and went over and sat beside her. They both sat there for a long moment without speaking.

"That was stupid. Getting involved."

"I wasn't going to just stand there and let that asshole shoot the deputy."

"You could've gotten yourself killed," Lilly said finally. To her surprise, she reached down and took his hand in hers. "It wasn't worth it."

He looked at her and saw something in her eyes that made him uncomfortable, but he didn't remove his hand.

"I've never killed anybody before. I did shoot a guy in the leg once. It's not the same."

"The guy you shot was a cold blooded shit bag," she assured him. "You didn't have a choice." She let go of his hand. "I'm just glad you're okay."

He didn't want her to let go of his hand and started to reach for it, but instead he got up from the bed and turned on the television. As he expected, the story was all over the news. A young blonde anchor woman was just beginning her report.

"Three police officers are dead and another was wounded at an incident at a home in northwest Houston."

A video showed the house surrounded by some half-dozen police cruisers. The camera panned away to show a figure draped by a white sheet lying in the middle of the street.

"The officers had just approached the house while investigating a report of an alleged arson. According to the sheriff's deputy who was wounded in the incident, the suspects immediately opened fire on the officers. The assailants are believed to be members of the White Liberation Front, a white supremacist street gang. Two of the assailants were also killed in the ensuing gun battle. One assailant escaped in what was reported to be an older model light blue van. Initial reports were that another assailant also escaped, possibly with a female hostage, although that has not been confirmed. The male assailant and the woman in question fled the scene in a white, late model Ford pickup with chrome wheels. An extensive police manhunt is ongoing. Police have attentively identified one of the suspects as Leroy Burns," she said as Burns' photo flashed on the screen. "Both of the escaped suspects should be considered armed and dangerous. More details on this story at five."

Soledad muted the TV. "So far there's no report of a bystander taking out one of them. I'm guessing they're keeping that quiet until they know more. Which means we've got some time. We need to ditch the other two guns and then figure out a way to get back to Mexico City."

"There's no reason why we can't fly back. You dye your hair and it shouldn't be a problem. There's no way they can connect us to this. All they've got is a blonde bystander saved a cop's life and then disappeared."

"I hope you're right," Soledad said, still not convinced. "Who wants to call Jeronimo and break the news?"

"You call. It sounds like a job for the head of Human Resources. What if he wants us to stay?"

"For what? If the cops catch up to Burns, Kate might very well end up as collateral damage. At best, they hold her for questioning until they sort it all out. Then it becomes Ranier's problem. Like you said, our job is over."

"Okay. You call him. I'm going to see Ranier."

"Why? I'm sure they told her what happened."

"I need to talk to her." Lilly picked p her handbag and started for the door, but then paused. "Did you know about Kate?"

"Know what?"

"That she's Jeronimo's granddaughter."

Soledad dropped back on the bed and looked at her. "Ranier told you that? And now I'm wondering if Jeronimo knew all along."

Lilly shrugged. "Ranier never told him."

"I should've known there was more to this. The question now is what he's going to want us to do."

"Don't call him until I get back. Okay?"

He nodded. He sat there after she left and thought. Lilly was right. There was really no point in calling him yet. Who knows? The cops would find Burns and it would all be decided for them. If not, then all bets were off.

illy parked on the edge of the lawn because a wrecker truck was in the process of loading one of the burned out cars onto a flatbed trailer. She sat there for a long moment trying to sort out her thoughts. Hattie Ranier's revelations earlier that morning, the unforeseen explosion of violence, and the equally unforeseen and brief feeling of intimacy she had felt towards Soledad all conspired to unsettle her. Reaching for his hand - what the hell was that about? Too much adrenaline and six, no almost seven years of celibacy, she thought. Allowing herself any sense of vulnerability or intimacy had gone by the wayside after they killed her lover Estevan in Culiácan. The last time she had felt anything remotely close to yearning had been the time spent with Harlan Quist after her escape from the prison. However, the precariousness of that situation had precluded her acting on any feeling she might have had for her old lover. And ever since arriving in Mexico City, she had kept to herself and remained guarded with her feelings.

She couldn't deny that she felt attracted to Soledad, but she still felt too unsure of herself to see it as anything but misguided fantasy. She realized that now was not the time for any complications. She put these thoughts aside and walked up to the porch.

Hattie Ranier must've seen her drive up for she was waiting with the door ajar. The morning's events had obviously taken its toll for her face appeared drawn and troubled.

"I'm guessing you've seen the news," Lilly said.

Ranier nodded. "The police called already and wanted to know again about Kate and how she had gotten involved with Burns and what their relationship was. I had to come clean and tell them she's my granddaughter."

"Did they ask if you had sent anyone to keep an eye on the house?"

"No. Why?"

"It's maybe better you don't know." Lilly hesitated. "But it'll come out soon enough that Soledad got involved. I'll leave it at that."

Ranier raised an eyebrow but said nothing.

"We're going back to Mexico City. I doubt there's anything we can do now."

"You've talked to him?"

"Jeronimo? Not yet. Have you thought anymore about telling him the truth?"

"I thought you suspected that he probably already knows."

"Well then that should make it easier. Call him. He needs to hear it from you, not me."

"So what happens now?" Ranier asked.

"Wait and see, I guess. The cops are bound to catch up with them. Let's just hope…" Lilly left it unsaid. "There's nothing else we can do." She tentatively placed her hand on Ranier's shoulder.

"I guess there's a lesson here," Ranier said, placing her hand on top of Lilly's. "About having faith in what will be."

"Acceptance, right? I guess you'll have to see if you can sell that to Jeronimo. Take care, Hattie."

"You too, Lilly," she said and closed the door.

PART TWO

"Living off the grid and being kind of an outlaw brings a dangerous reality."

- Ron Perlman

VILLA GROVE, COLORADO

Two Months Later

Kate flung off the sleeping bag and rose up on one elbow. What passed for daylight leaked from below the edge of the tattered blanket that served as a curtain covering the bedroom window. Se swung her feet onto the cold linoleum floor and glanced over her shoulder at Leroy who stirred momentarily, grunted, and pulled his pillow over his head. She lingered there for a moment before leaning down and scooping up her sweat pants, a denim work shirt, and the grungy wool socks that doubled as slippers. The small, anemic electric space heater had overheated and shut off sometime during the night. She slipped on her clothes, unplugged the heater, and carried it with her out into the front room of the small trailer. The room consisted of a rudimentary kitchen and what passed for a dining and living room. She had been in department store changing rooms that were larger.

She walked over to the dinner plate- sized sink, parted the thin curtain, and peered out at the morning. The gray, lowering sky had started to spit snow. Here it was late March and the only sign of impending spring was that the roads were muddy rather than snow-packed. That and the fact they no longer had to wrap the trailer's door handle with a towel to keep it from freezing up at night.

She thought about Hattie's yard back in Houston, and how the roses and azaleas would be in full bloom. She could close her eyes and visualize the sea of bluebonnets in the file behind Hattie's house, and almost smell the funky, warm breeze wafting from the nearby bayou.

She caught sight of Sunny Dalton leading her horse out of the stable. Kate was confident Dalton would have something to say about the fact that they hadn't been up to feed the horses and muck the stalls. Sure enough, Dalton cast a disparaging glance in the direction of the trailer before swinging up into the saddle.

Kate muttered a curse and switched on the small hot plate. Only then did she remember that they were out of instant coffee. She cursed again and slammed the flimsy cabinet door violently enough to almost rip it from its hinges. She was done with this, she decided for the tenth time in two days.

The night before, she and Leroy engaged in their usual tense exchange about when they might have enough money saved up to escape their current fate. Tired of Kate's grumbling, Leroy had sarcastically suggested they hike the four miles to the highway and thumb a ride. To fucking where had been her angry rejoinder.

They had fled north into Colorado with the intention of seeking refuge with Leroy's cousin in Montana. The cousin, himself one small step removed from their own criminal predicament, had offered them a spare room until they figured out their next move.

They had arrived in Villa Grove penniless, their last reserves of cash spent filling their gas tank in Alamosa. At that point, their meager hoard of food consisted of half of a case of canned tuna, a handful of energy bars, and a sack of oranges. A chance encounter with Caleb Dalton at the Villa Grove Trade had resulted in his offer of employment and a place to stay. Little did they know that his offer had less to do with goodwill than the Dalton's need for a source of cheap labor.

The trailer where they had encamped belonged to the Daltons, a mother and son, neither of whom Lilly came to realize possessed a charitable bone in their body. The mother, Sunny, was a harpy if there ever was one. Her miscreant son Caleb was a shiftless lout who spent the day smoking pot and doing little else. Despite the Dalton's obvious wealth, they paid Kate and Leroy fifty dollars a week plus free room in exchange for feeding their horses and cleaning their stalls. Or at least they were supposed to pay them that, for any semblance of a salary required Leroy to constantly pester Caleb to pay up. Consequently, they felt themselves to be a notch above indentured servants.

In the meantime, they subsisted on whatever they could scrounge. The week before, Leroy had bought a fifty-pound sack of potatoes and some onions and pinto beans at a roadside stand. They hoped it would supplement the haunch of elk venison they had bought from a hunter selling poached game out of the back of a pickup. The elk meat was already turning gamey with the warmer days. Their situation grew more dire by the day and had metastasized into a bitter bone of contention between the two of them.

She heard the toilet flush, and a moment later Leroy shuffled out of the bedroom. She stiffened when he came up behind her and wrapped his arms around her waist.

"Coffee ready?"

"We're out," she said, not bothering to conceal her irritation.

He mumbled something unintelligible and reached past her to part the curtains. "I say we go into Villa Grove and treat ourselves to a latte and some of those banana muffins."

"What? Caleb finally paid us?"

"He coughed up fifty," he replied, stepping back from the window.

"Fifty? That's all? That suck ass owes us for three weeks," she exclaimed.

"It's coming. And more than just what he owes us."

"What do you mean?"

"I'll tell you later. Get dressed and let's get some coffee. I'll go and get the car warm."

They had traded Leroy's almost new, tricked-out, F-150 truck for a beat-up Toyota Celica at a roadside mechanic's garage outside of Houston. The garage owner knew not to ask questions. As an added precaution, Leroy stole some license plates from an abandoned car parked in a derelict gas station.

Kate slipped on a sweatshirt and then bundled her threadbare sweater around her before joining Leroy in the muddy yard. She had found the sweater abandoned in a gas station rest room in Alamosa. They had foolishly neglected to buy anything remotely suitable for a winter in the Rockies. Both had been born and bred on the Texas coast, where winter meant rain and the rare frost on your windshield in the morning.

As they started to drive off, Caleb Dalton emerged from the stable and waved them down. He wore a pair of camouflaged overalls and a Denver Bronco's gimme cap, his attire completed by the holstered handgun he always wore around his waist.

"Where are you all going?" he asked after Leroy lowered his window. "The stalls need cleaning."

He bent and leaned through the window and offered them his rank, dog's breath. He had the kind of unremarkable face that one would struggle to recall fifteen minutes after meeting him. He always had the same, loopy, all-weather smile that was partially concealed by a thick, auburn-colored beard. His dark, dime-sized eyes reflected all the intelligence of a rodent. Kate abhorred him as much as she did his mother.

"We'll get to it. We're going for coffee first," Leroy explained. He started to roll up the window, but Caleb leaned in closer.

"My Mom wants an answer today. Understand?"

"Yeah, got it," Leroy replied and pulled away before Caleb could say anything more.

"What was that all about?"

He didn't reply or much less look at her. She studied him. He had grown a beard and allowed his hair to grow past his shoulders. It made him look even more like some forlorn derelict. She wondered for the fiftieth time in the last two months what she had ever seen in him. Granted, he treated her decently and was still ruggedly handsome in a shopworn way, but his silver-tongued charm had fallen by the wayside within an hour of fleeing Houston. Running from the law with every cop in the state looking for you could do that, she figured. And it wasn't as if she was still an eyeful.

"They know about us," he said as he rolled down his window to hit the button to open the gate. "Don't ask me how, but that paranoid, scheming bitch found out somehow. And now they want us to help them. And if we don't… Well, they could turn us in. There's bound to be reward money."

"Wait. Help them do what?"

"There's this old guy that has the next ranch over between here and Villa Grove. I guess the Dalton's have been trying to buy him out, but so far he hasn't taken them up on their offer. He must've told them he didn't need their dirty money."

"Dirty money? What did he mean by that?"

Leroy shrugged. "Who knows? Anyway, it seems the old guy used to have this housekeeper, a Mexican woman that Caleb must've been screwing. She told Caleb that the old guy keeps a suitcase full of cash squirreled away under the floorboards in his kitchen. The housekeeper was going to take it for herself, but the old guy got pissed at her for something and called INS on her. So now Caleb and his mother have it in their minds to relieve him of that suitcase. Force his hand to sell then his place."

"And they want us to help them? Have you lost your mind? We're already neck deep in the shit. I'm not doing it. I'd rather turn myself in now and take my chances."

"Look, it's not like we're knocking off a bank for chrissakes."

"No, we're just helping them rob some old man of his life savings.'

"The old guy must be well off. He owns lots of land. Robbing him isn't going to leave hum destitute or anything."

"I don't care. I'm not doing it. You hear me? I won't."

"Okay. Then I guess we better run," he said softly. "They're not gonna take no for an answer. So we go back to the trailer, get our gear and leave tonight."

"And go where? And how far will we get before they set the cops on us? Are you forgetting we hardly have a hundred bucks to our name?"

"That's exactly why we need to do this. Say we help him. Wait," he said when she started to protest. "Hear me out. Our cut will be half. We'll have enough to get us to Mexico and a fresh start."

"And when that money runs out? God, Leroy. Living like this is a dead end. Don't you see that? I can't do this anymore. Did you hear me? I'm done," she shouted when he didn't say anything.

"Do you have some kind of plan in mind or are you just running off your mouth?" he said softly, his eyes never leaving the road.

"You're a loser, you know that?"

He finally looked at her. "And what pray tell leads you to think you're not?" When she didn't reply, he went on. "Has it ever occurred to you that maybe we've both reached our highest station in life?"

She cuffed him on the ear hard enough that he almost ran off the road into a bar ditch. He slammed on the brakes and skidded to a stop on the side of the road. He reached up and rubbed his ear.

"What the hell?" He looked at his hand to check for blood.

You fucking asshole! I should've never let you drag me out of that house. I could've…"

"Stayed behind and let the cops shoot you? You know well and well that's what would've happened. You kill a cop in Texas, hell anywhere, and it is open season."

She shook her head but said nothing.

"Whether you like it or not, we're in this together."

'Until death do us part. Is that it?"

He reached over and placed his hand on her shoulder. "I'm sorry."

She pushed his hand away. "Tomorrow you take me to Alamosa. They have an airport there, don't they? I'm going back to Houston."

He snorted in amusement. "How are getting on a plane? You don't even have an ID, much less money for a ticket."

A long moment of silence passed before she finally said, "See you, Leroy." She tried to open the door but it was stuck. "Goddammit!" she shrieked in frustration.

He reached across her and took her hand off the door handle. "I'm not leaving you out here."

She leaned her head against the cold window. She already knew the answer. They would do it. She would do it. And they would run again.

He pulled back onto the highway. They drove the rest of the way to Villa Grove in silence.

They pulled up in front of the Villa Grove Trade and Leroy cut the ignition. The place was more of a diner and coffee shop than anything resembling a convenience store. It was a narrow, ramshackle building with a false front like what you saw in photos and movies of old timey Western towns. However, the interior contrasted with its rundown looking exterior. The inside was homey, pleasantly decorated, and served an assortment of pastries and food. In summer, one could even dine in an outdoor garden out back.

"You get us some coffee. I'm going to walk down to the Sugar Shack and get a six-pack," Leroy said, forcing open the rusty driver's s side door. The Sugar Shack was a small makeshift liquor store a short walk away.

"Are you forgetting that I need money?"

He reached into his shirt pocket, pulled out a thin sheaf of bills, and handed them to her. She snatched them from him before he could change his mind and stuffed the cash into the pocket of her sweater. He crawled out and set out down the road.

She took a quick glance at what he had given her- a ten and three ones. Two lattes and some muffins would use up most of it. She looked up to see an old woman wearing what looked to be three layers of threadbare clothes walk out of the shop and make her way to her truck. The woman's feet were encased in a pair of mismatched, mud-caked rubber galoshes. Kate wondered if a stranger might view her own pitiful attire with the same empathy. She pushed these thoughts aside and made her way into the store.

She walked up to the cashier, a thin, sallow older woman with carrot-colored hair. Her ever-cheerful demeanor belied her hard-bitten, weathered appearance. The woman offered her a wide grin, exposing her yellow, nicotine-stained teeth.

"Hi. Could I have a couple of lattes, please?"

The woman smiled. "Anything else?"

"I'll take a couple of banana muffins."

"I'm sorry it's so cold in here," the woman said. "The heater's on the blink."

Kate nodded and glanced up at the wide-screen television mounted on the wall. It was broadcasting an episode of The Price Is Right. No such thing as the right price, she thought bitterly.

"Could I have the key to the ladies' room, please?

The cashier reached behind her and lifted a key off a hook. "Gonna be cold as a witch's tit in there. Careful your behind don't freeze to the seat."

Kate took the key, nodded and started to turn away.

"You're stayin' out at the Dalton place, aren't you?" the woman asked.

Kate turned and looked at her. "How did you know?" she asked, giving into her curiosity.

"Your boyfriend told me as much. Plus, it's a small world up here in this valley. Everyone knows your business. You know what I mean? It can't be the greatest place to winter," she added. "I've seen that trailer where you're stayin'. It must be cold this time of year."

No shit, Kate wanted to say, but instead nodded and retreated to the restroom. She reminded herself to tell Leroy that he best keep his mouth shut about where they were staying.

The cashier was right. It was too cold to sit on the toilet seat. She peed, and despite the cold, sat there a moment pondering her predicament. She rummaged in her belt bag in the hope she had misplaced some cash. There were a couple of one dollar bills and a folded paper towel. Wrapped inside the towel, she found half of a long forgotten joint and a half-used book of matches. She shook her head in appreciation, lit a match, pinched the joint between her fingers, and took a puff. She paused and took two more hits before dropping the roach into the toilet.

At the sink, she washed her hands and studied herself in the grimy mirror. She thought about the cashier and wondered what kind of hard choices the woman had made in her life to merit her appearance and her current station in life. Was the woman a harbinger of her own future? If so, she was off to a good start, she thought as she peered closer at her image in the mirror. The skin of her face appeared dry and chapped, her hair brittle and lifeless thanks to the once-a-week shampoo using the bar soap and the cold alkaline well water.

She couldn't go on this way. She was almost willing to turn herself in and take her chances. At least in jail there would be hot showers. All it would take would be for her to walk into the police station in Salida or Alamosa and tell them she was on the FBI's Most Wanted List; the payoff being a warm cot, hot coffee, and a shower. Hattie would help her find a lawyer. Or was that merely wishful thinking? After what had happened in Houston, her grandmother had washed her hands of her.

She stared at herself a moment longer and started to turn away before hesitating. There might be another way. She dug into her belt bag and took out what remained of the nub of lipstick she hadn't used in two months; any sense of vanity having long ago fallen by the wayside. She thought for a moment and then swiped the smudge and fog from the mirror and began to carefully scrawl.

Call Hattie 713-662-4407. Tel her I'm ready to come home.

She tossed what remained of the lipstick in the trash and walked out. She handed the woman the cash, and as she waited for her change, glanced out the window at Leroy who stood leaning against the car. She would run and take her chances without him, she decided.

"Thanks," she said, taking her change and stuffing it in the pocket of her jeans. "Oh, and you you might want to check the restroom. You're out of paper towels." She smiled and walked out.

By the time they reached the trailer, it had started to drizzle, a mix of fine rain and sleet. The Dalton's Range Rover sat parked in front of the trailer. They sat in silence for a moment after Leroy cut the ignition.

"I guess it's time to shit or get off the pot," he said softly.

She grunted as she joined him in his thoughts before forcing open her door. "Let's get this over with," she said.

She smelled them the moment she opened the trailer door. The small, cramped living and kitchen area smelled of Sunny Dalton's patchouli and the funky perfume of Caleb's rank body odor. He stood leaning against the kitchen counter with his arms crossed while his mother had settled at the small, badly chipped, Formica-topped table. Other than the table, the only other furnishings in the trailer's small living area were a trio of frayed nylon lawn chairs and a sagging soiled sofa. The cramped one bedroom held little more than a grimy mattress on a rickety double bed, a lamp without a shade and an unpainted chest of drawers.

Sunny Dalton was petite and buxom, and Kate guessed that some men might find her appealing in the same way one might find some kind of exotic and dangerous animal worthy of consideration. Her helmet of curly, dirty blonde hair framed an angular face with high cheek bones and an even higher forehead. She had deep-set, China-blue eyes and a knife-like mouth with thin lips that were curled in perpetual disdain.

It was difficult to guess her age because her pale skin showed little signs of blemish or wrinkles. Somewhere between fifty and sixty she thought gauging from the age of her half-wit offspring. On first meeting her, Kate found her initial cordial demeanor forced and off-putting, if not oddly menacing.

Caleb Dalton bore little resemblance to his mother in either his facial features or body type, making one wonder whether they were even related, or Caleb was merely the spawn of the devil.

For once, it was hot in the trailer, and Kate suspected the Daltons had cranked up the small, propane stove that served as the trailer's only other source of heat besides the small electric space heater which they usually kept in the bedroom.

"Kids," Sunny Dalton said, holding her arms out in greeting.

She sat at the small Formica table with an insulted coffee mug at her elbow. She looked past Kate at Leroy for a few seconds before setting her eyes on Kate.

"So, Leroy. You've spoken with her?" Her voice was reedy with a curious sing-song quality. She kept her eyes fixed on Kate before finally turning her gaze back on Leroy.

"Why don't you ask me?" Kate said before Leroy could reply.

Dalton looked back at Kate. "For being so young, you're quite the little…"

"Bitch?"

Her smile seemed to darken. "I was going to say hard ass, but bitch works. So, are you in on this or not?"

Kate walked over to the table and pulled out one of the plastic lawn chairs and sat down across from her.

"Tell us exactly what you've got planned. Then I'll tell you if we're in," Kate answered, not feeling her bravado.

Dalton smiled in amusement and looked back again at Leroy.

"She's the one you've gotta convince," Leroy said.

"I already told you," Caleb cut in. "The money's in a suitcase under the kitchen floorboards. The housekeeper seen it once when the old guy was puttin' money in it. Catanach's got…"

His mother's hand shot up to silence him and she shot him a cold look of reproach.

"The old fart," she went on. "Has a woman he sees in Alamosa every Friday. That's four days from now. So, we wait until he leaves, and then we go in and take the suitcase. No one to stop us. No gunplay or drama. It's a simple case of burglary."

"There's no one else living on the property?" Leroy interjected. "Ranch hands? No neighbors nearby?"

"Nope."

"Guard dog?"

Caleb Dalton shook his head. "Least ways not outside. I drove up there to the house once just to case it out. I never seen no dog."

"So what do you need us for?" Kate asked Sunny Dalton whose eyes had never left Kate.

"A simple matter of efficiency more than anything," she replied, taking a sip of her coffee. "For one, there's no telling how much of that kitchen floor we'll have to rip up. That and we might need someone to keep an eye out. Like I said, the old guy goes to Alamosa. Most times he doesn't come back until late the next morning. But one never knows for sure."

Dalton took another sip of her coffee before going on. "I understand you two are planning on leaving here soon anyway. That makes it cleaner. I can't have any local talent involved. I'm guessing by the time he discovers his money's gone, you two will be cooling your jets on a beach somewhere."

"How much money are we talking about?" Leroy asked.

"We're not entirely sure," Caleb said. "The housekeeper just said this suitcase was packed tight with piles of money. From what I can tell, Catanach hasn't spent a red nickel keeping up that ranch or the house for that matter. The place is a dump."

"So where did he get all his cash?" Leroy asked.

"The cheap bastard's most likely been squirreling it away for years," Caleb answered. "We figure he's one of those types that don't trust the banks."

Sunny Dalton looked at each of them in turn. When neither of them said anything, she stood and picked up her coffee mug.

"We'll sleep on it," Kate said.

Dalton stared at Kate for a long moment before casting her gaze on Leroy. "Okay. I expect an answer in the morning. Just be aware that if your answer is no, then I'm expecting you two to vacate the premises forthwith. I can't have any heat coming down on my place after this goes down." She offered Leroy a cold, hard glance and walked past him and out the door. Caleb followed her without saying anything.

"I don't trust them. They're snakes," Kate said without looking back at Leroy who still stood beside the door.

"Then we best be careful where we step," he said, settling into the chair across from her. He popped open one of the Coors and handed it to her.

"I'm sorry I called you a loser," she said, taking a sip of the beer.

"Well, we sure as hell aren't winners, are we? Not yet at least," he added. "When this is over, I'll make it up to you. I promise. I'll get us to Mexico or Costa Rica."

She handed him the can of beer. "They must take us for idiots. We're supposed to help him dig up the floor. He gives us our share. And then we disappear. I don't like the disappear part. It sounds a little too convenient. Like the housekeeper suddenly getting fired and scooped up by immigration."

"I thought of that, too. Yeah, I don't trust either of them either."

"So, what do we do?"

Leroy took a swallow of beer and considered the question. "What we do is help them dig up that floor. And then we turn the tables. What're they gonna do? Call the cops? Babe, we're already outlaws on the run. We might as well run with a pocketful of spending money."

Lilly thought for a moment. Money would get her to Houston. Maybe even pay for a lawyer. And what about Leroy? Despite the fact he had been fun and had always treated her well, it was time they both moved on. He would do fine in Mexico. But she had no intention of going with him.

"It's warm in here for a change," she said, looking at him evenly. The two hits of weed had stirred her libido. "Almost warm enough to take off our clothes."

"That's another thought that crossed my mind." He set down his beer, got up, and came up behind her. He stroked her one cheek. His hands were cool from the beer, but she could feel the warmth of his body as he bent over to nuzzle her neck. She leaned into him and craned her neck up to kiss him.

She stood up and began discarding the layers of her clothes one by one – the filthy sweater, the denim work shirt, the grimy cargo pants, the tattered long underwear - until she stood before him nude.

He studied her for a moment before stripping off his own clothes. It had been weeks since they had engaged in sex. The cold, their neglected hygiene, and their desperation had blunted their desire for one another. And now here they were, their spurious, corrupt passion reignited by the prospect of robbing an old man of his life's savings. It bothered her and yet it didn't, she thought as she watched Leroy kick off his jeans.

Perhaps, this was her kharma - the fate that Hattie would always warn her about. And she felt helpless to change it. She, Leroy, the Daltons, the old rancher, they were all part of her kharma. She pushed these thoughts from her mind as she took Leroy by the hand and led him to the sofa.

MEXICO CITY
Two Days Later

Lilly studied herself in the bathroom mirror as she attempted to button the waistband of her trousers. She should have had them altered rather than simply settling for purchasing them off the rack. Or she should have been eating out less and spending more time at the gym. She sucked in her stomach and fastened the last button. If she could wear her blouse loose and not tucked in it wouldn't be a problem, but the trousers were part of a business suit.

The trousers were a dove-colored, linen-wool blend with a matching jacket in a darker shade of gray. She couldn't ever recall wearing an outfit remotely as chic. Purchasing it had been at Jeronimo's urging. He had tasked her with attending a business meeting in Guadalajara later that day and expected her to look professional.

Jeronimo had recently acquired one third interest in a tequila distillery in Jalisco. It seemed another of his attempts to achieve a measure of legitimacy. The other two partners were an American movie actor and a young tech entrepreneur from Monterrey. Jeronimo's instructions were for her to simply deliver some papers for signing and then to sit in on a meeting with the other two partners. He explicitly instructed her to say nothing. She was not to make comments or offer any input, but only to observe and afterwards offer him her impressions of his new partners. But he insisted that this meeting required a serious outfit, thus the business suit.

She slipped on the white silk blouse and tucked it into the waist band. Not so bad if she kept the jacket buttoned. Out of the corner of her eye, she noticed Soledad watching her from the doorway. He was wearing her silk dressing gown with the sash half-open, revealing the fact he wore nothing underneath it.

"You look nice," he remarked. *"Muy elegante."*

"And you look like some kind of sorry excuse for a drag queen," she replied. "Where's that robe I bought you last week?"

He shrugged and fingered the robe. "I like this. *Muy elegante.*"

"More like *muy ridícula,*" she said, dabbing away some lipstick from the corner of her mouth.

He looked at his watch. "You're going to be late. Hilario's downstairs having a fit."

"I've got time. There's never much traffic on Sunday morning. Why don't you call Hilario and tell him to come up and grab a cup of coffee?" she asked playfully.

"Oh yeah. I'm sure he'd give Jeronimo an earful."

"Especially if he sees you in my robe. Do you really think the boss doesn't suspect anything? The all-knowing Jeronimo Hermosa, the man with spies on every street corner?"

"If he does, he keeps it close to the vest as usual."

She stepped back from the mirror and took a final look at herself before reaching for her jacket. "Someone's phone is ringing. Yours's or mine?"

"Mine," he replied, walking back into the bedroom.

She heard him engage in a short conversation before turning to look at her as she stepped into the bedroom. He had an obvious look of amusement on his face.

"What?"

"That was the boss," he said, slipping on his underwear. "He wants to see us right away."

"Us?"

"Yeah. He said if you hadn't left yet to bring you along."

She smiled and shook her head. "Well, so much for our discretion."

Twenty minutes later, Hilario dropped them off at Jeronimo's mansion. Perhaps because it was Sunday, for once there wasn't an armed guard at his door. As usual, Maria opened the door before they had even mounted the stairs. Maria nodded and turned to lead them inside. As was her custom, Lilly paused to exchange a few words with Bruno, the macaw, before hurrying to catch up with Soledad who gave a perfunctory knock on Jeronimo's office door before entering.

As soon as Lilly stepped through the threshold, she sensed that something seemed out of place. For one thing, Jeronimo wasn't sitting behind his desk as was his usual custom. It took a moment for her to spot him standing in his solarium. And he wasn't alone. She immediately recognized his companion. The orange robe, the shaved head. It could only be one person. Lilly glanced at Soledad whose expression reflected his own surprise.

"Oh oh," she muttered.

Jeronimo must have sensed their arrival, for he turned and gestured with his arm for Hattie to step back into the office. As Hattie stepped inside, she smiled at Lilly, but merely nodded at Soledad. Jeronimo slipped behind his desk without greeting them.

"This is a surprise," Lilly offered, her gaze moving from Hattie to Jeronimo and then back to Hattie as she attempted to ascertain what might have transpired between them.

"No doubt," Hattie said simply.

Lilly could only assume that some accord had been reached between the two of them, the necessary disclosures had been made, and some kind of polite détente achieved. Though Lilly couldn't imagine how such a thing as an affair gone wrong with a resulting unacknowledged progeny could fail to generate a measure of appreciable heat. As usual, Jeronimo's demeanor revealed nothing.

"Let me guess. There's a development," Lilly hazarded to say.

Hattie took a seat on the sofa and glanced at Jeronimo before replying.

"Two nights ago, I received a phone call from a woman. She had a strange message. She called from a place called Villa Grove, Colorado. She works at some sort of a café or a store. A trading post is what she called it. A young woman wrote a message on the mirror in the restroom instructing someone to call me. It said quote unquote, I'm ready to come home.'"

"Kate?"

"I can only assume. Who else would leave my number?"

"This woman. Did she offer a description?" Soledad asked.

"From what she said…. Yes. It sounded like it was Kate."

"Where is this Villa Grove place anyway?" Lilly asked, sitting down beside Hattie.

"Central Colorado. The middle of nowhere. Do you know Colorado?"

"No. Not at all," Lilly replied.

"I went hunting there once," Soledad offered. "Up outside of Durango. Did this woman say anything else? About where Kate might be?"

"Only that she might be living in a trailer out at some nearby ranch."

Lilly looked at Jeronimo. "Something tells me I'm not going to Guadalajara."

"I've already taken care of that. It can wait." He folded his hands in front of his mouth for a few seconds as if collecting his thoughts. "There are no longer any secrets here. Do you understand?" he asked, looking at Lilly and Soledad in turn. "What I want… what we want," he said, glancing at Hattie. "Is that this matter will be picked up where it was left. Do I make myself clear?"

Lilly looked up at Soledad who was leaning against the wall off to the side. He met her gaze briefly and straightened.

"We go after her," he said simply, more a statement than a question.

"I want her taken out of harm's way," Hattie said, her eyes locked on Jeronimo. The tone of her voice left no doubt that this wasn't a request.

"I have already made certain arrangements and inquiries," Jeronimo said. "You will leave for Houston this afternoon. You will be met there by my representative who has arranged for a private jet to fly you to Colorado. A town called Alamosa. She will arrange everything else. A vehicle and whatever else you might require."

"We bring Kate back to Houston?" Lilly asked, glancing first at Hattie and then at Jeronimo.

"No," Jeronimo said. "You will bring her here." He looked at Hattie. "We have agreed it is for the best."

Hattie nodded in agreement. No one said anything for a long moment. Jeronimo finally broke the silence. "I hope there will not be any complications."

He was obviously referring to what occurred in Houston. The day after arriving back in Mexico City, she and Soledad met with Jeronimo for a debriefing. Their account included everything but Lilly's private conversations with Hattie, and of course the incident with the Jamaican, although Lilly had no doubt word of the encounter had filtered back to Jeronimo. Soledad had left out nothing in regard to the shootout at the house.

She and Soledad had followed the story regarding the shooting in the Houston newspapers for several days after returning. It wasn't until five days later that a follow-up article appeared in the Houston Chronicle. It stated that the surviving sheriff's deputy was recovering from his wounds, and that there still had not been any progress in locating the assailants that had fled the scene. The police had also been unable to identify the bystander who had shot and killed one of the assailants and undoubtedly saved the life of the wounded deputy.

It was at about this same time that Soledad had found his way into Lilly's bed, and the rest as they say, was history. It wasn't unexpected, nor was it unwanted. It just happened, and for now at least, they both rode with it.

Lilly got to her feet. "I'll bring her back. I promise." She stood and started for the door. Soledad started to follow her.

"*Esperar*, Jaime," Jeronimo said. "*Necesito una palabra.*"

"Okay. I'll meet you outside," Lilly said, turning to the door. Hattie rose to her feet and followed her.

"So, I'm guessing you told him. Or did he already know?" Lilly added as Hattie joined her in the hallway.

Hattie offered a slight smile. "He suspected Kate and I had some kind of relationship. But no, he didn't know about Kate's mother. That he had sired a child all those years ago."

"And how did he take it?"

She shrugged. "As you know, Jeronimo is not the kind to reveal his feelings that easily. It was always one of our problems. But he and I have history. One with a great deal of passion and fondness. And yes, heart ache. As is sometimes the case, it is the passion and fondness that burns the brightest and longest." She paused a moment before going on.

"There is still reconciliation to be done. Explanations and I'm sure recriminations. But I am hopeful."

"And you're all right with Kate coming here?"

"I'm afraid she doesn't have anything waiting for her in Texas but a prison cell. Here…" She shrugged. "Maybe a chance at something different."

Lilly wanted to assure her that some sort of redemption was possible. Look at me she wanted to say, even though running errands for a crime boss wasn't exactly what Hattie was likely envisioning for Kate.

"How long are you staying?" Lilly asked.

"Just until I know she's safe." She took Lilly's hands in hers and placed them onto her chest. "Be careful," she said, clutching Lilly's hands for a moment longer before turning and returning to Jeronimo's study.

Soledad emerged a few seconds later. "Are you ready for this?"

"What did he want?" she asked, ignoring his question.

Soledad smiled. "Just some unfinished personnel problems. You know, human resources stuff."

She could tell he was being less than honest but decided to confront him about it later.

"Do you have any warm clothes?" he asked. "I've heard springtime in the Rockies can be brutal."

"Then you'd better take me shopping," she said and started down the hallway.

PART THREE

"Many commit the same crime with a different destiny; one bears a cross as the price of villainy while another wears a crown."

-the Roman poet Juvenal

COLORADO

Lilly toweled her hair dry and then brushed her teeth. It had been nearly midnight and the end of a long day before they reached their motel room in Alamosa. Giving into exhaustion, she had collapsed into bed without even undressing. The sound of an alarm clock going off in the adjacent motel room had awakened her at six. Unable to return to sleep, she slipped out of bed and spent a good twenty minutes under the shower.

She was just grateful Jeronimo had hired a private jet to take them to Alamosa. If they would've relied on a commercial flight, they would have had to spend the night in Houston, prolonging the trip by a day. True to his word, Jeronimo had arranged for them to be met after clearing immigration and customs in Houston. His representative, an attractive young Latina by the name if Mariposa, had shepherded them to the waiting Lear jet. She told them someone else would meet their plane in Alamosa and provide them with a vehicle and anything else they might need.

From what she had read about Alamosa, it was in a high, windswept valley and was notorious for being one of the coldest cities in the lower forty-eight. The town itself seemed to have little to offer other than a small state college and an abundance of outdoor activities. The surrounding countryside was mostly ranch and farm country.

The temperature was grazing thirty when they landed, and the wind was gusting hard enough to require one to walk with one's head down. She was just glad she was able on short notice to find a down jacket, insulted boots, and a pair of fleece-lined wind pants in Mexico City. She had also purchased a set of flannel sweats. It made her recall how she had once worn nothing but flannels and camouflage while living the life of the paramour of the leader of a white nationalist militia in Idaho. Another time and another life, she thought. Just another one of the incarnations she had tried to put behind her.

The person who greeted them in Alamosa was not as attractive or gracious as Mariposa. The man was burly, unshaven, and irritable. He went out of his way twice to mention he had driven all the way down from Denver. It was obvious from his expensive looking loafers and rumpled business suit that it was unlikely he was a mere delivery boy.

Like the accountant he might have been, the man from Denver unlocked the compartment in the bed of a used, extended cab Dodge pickup and meticulously catalogued the list of provisions that Jeronimo had requested.

His recitation included maps, flashlights, a pair of binoculars, a first aid kit, thermoses, a tool kit, a pair of night vision glasses, two Kevlar vests, a pair of Glocks, what he referred to as a tactical shotgun, and the appropriate ammunition for their arsenal. The man made a point of telling them the serial numbers on the three weapons had been removed. The armaments made Lilly uneasy about what they might be encountering. The gun battle in Houston had obviously led Soledad to err on the side of caution as he had once put it.

After she finished drying her hair, she went back into the bedroom and slipped in beside Soledad. He didn't stir until she curled up against his back.

"Coffee," he whispered hoarsely without turning over.

"No coffee, but will you settle for a little half and half?"

He rolled over and looked at her. "Uh, half and half? What do you mean?"

She flung off the covers. "It's something I learned in prison. Mind you, in theory only," she added.

"But I gather you can demonstrate."

"I sure can Roll over on your back."

An hour and a half later, Soledad stood hunched against the wind in front of a food truck. The wind had grown fiercer, kicking up several swirling dust devils in the empty, unpaved parking lot. As he waited for their coffee and burritos, he turned and looked back at Lilly who sat waiting in the truck.

She was proving to be even more complicated than he originally anticipated. And more vexing. And more intoxicating. It had been several years since he had been in any relationship that rose to the level of intimacy and unremitting challenges that Lilly offered. She was dangerous in more ways than one; unpredictable, even volatile, and surely addictive. And now he wondered if it had been a mistake on Jeronimo's part to have her accompany him. In retrospect, he should've raised an objection. But then he had to ask himself if any objection was colored by his concern for her welfare. In the back of his mind, he also couldn't help but consider the possibility that any violent encounter might affect their relationship in some unintended and unpredictable way. Violence had its consequences and it affected people differently. From what Jeronimo had shared, Lilly was certainly no stranger to violence. Still, it was the fallout that might prove to be the wild card.

He tried to put these thoughts aside as he carried their breakfast back to the truck. She murmured her thanks and they pulled out onto the highway and headed north. Villa Grove was nothing more than a stop in the road and only about fifty miles away. They drank their coffee and ate their burritos in silence as they watched the town give way to scrubby brush land.

"So, are you going to tell me what Jeronimo said to you after I left his office?" she asked, licking her fingers.

He glanced at her but didn't reply. He balled up the wrapper of the burrito and tossed it onto the dash, then took a sip of coffee.

"He told me not to come back without her, and to do what we had to do."

"And I suppose that's the reason for the arsenal. I'm not shooting anyone, Jaime. You hear me?"

"I'll hold you to that," he remarked with obvious sarcasm. "Look, I don't think it'll come to that."

A moment passed before he said, "He also said that you might be too invested."

"Invested? What the shit is that supposed to mean?" she asked, her sudden flare of anger catching him off guard.

He paused a moment before replying. "I guess he's wondering if you're identifying too much with Kate. You know, because of your background."

"My background?"

"Look, I have to confess that there are things he told me about you. This was even before we ever went to Houston. I should've told you," He added.

"Fuck him. I don't know," she said after a moment. "Maybe he's right. Maybe I am too invested."

"He still thinks you're just what might be needed. Remember what he said before about this needing a woman's touch?"

Another long moment of silence followed before she said "My background, huh? Yeah, I had a shitty childhood. My mother abandoned me when I was ten. This was right after my sorry excuse for a father got sent up for the second time for holding up a grocery store. I ended up living on the streets for a while. Then it was a half-dozen or so foster homes. I spent a year in juvie for stealing a TV. Did he tell you I've done time twice? The last time was for robbing an armored car." She drank the last of her coffee and dropped the cup on the floorboard. "Did he tell you I probably killed somebody?"

"What do you mean probably?"

She looked at him and met his gaze. "Okay. I've killed somebody. More than just one. Please don't ask. At least I didn't shoot anybody in Houston," she said in response to his look of surprise.

He was thinking about how close she had come to shooting the Jamaican. That was the problem. What would happen the next time? Maybe that was what Jeronimo was worried about.

"Yeah," she said after a moment. "The road to perdition. Isn't that what your daddy called it? I guess I do know that road. And Kate's already taken the on ramp."

He looked at her after a long moment had passed. "I don't give a shit about your past."

"I do. Here I thought I had been born again, that I had a chance at a different kind if life, and then Jeronimo gets me involved in something like this."

"I just need to know about who you are now. Forget about the past. Of course, that doesn't mean I want you to forget about that half and half stuff," he said with a smile.

"You liked that, did you?"

"I'll never think of coffee the same way," he replied.

She turned on the radio and began surfing the stations. They were mostly country western with a few Christian talk radio programs thrown in. She finally found a station out of Denver that played contemporary rock. She turned up the volume and the singer, a woman, was lamenting,

"Will we burn in heaven? Like we do down here?"

"Funny. I've wondered about that very same thing," she murmured. They drove in silence for a while before she asked, "Are you thinking there's a real possibility we're going to get into some kind of a shootout?"

He shrugged. "I hope not. Kate said she wanted out. That should make it easier. But we have no idea what her situation really is. Or who this Leroy Burns character has them hooked up with."

They again fell into an easy silence as the countryside rolled by. The landscape had grown more arid, the dusty, treeless plain giving way to an endless carpet of sage brush interrupted by the occasional fallow field. The San Luis Valley was broad and flat, and gauging from the map, it ran for some hundred and twenty miles before it ran up against the mountains. To the east rose a chain of high, rugged, snow-capped peaks. The map indicated the mountains ranged from twelve to fourteen thousand feet in elevation. The Sangre de Cristos they were called. The Blood of Christ - so named by the early Spanish settlers when they first saw the snowy mountains turned blood red by the setting sun. The valley was a lonely looking place with sparse habitation.

They passed a sign heralding the cutoff to the Great Sand Dunes National Park. Sure enough, in the distance they could see a huge expanse of high, treeless, dune-colored hills cradled against the craggy peaks. A little later, they passed a sign bearing the silhouette of an alligator and announcing 'Alligator Farm'. A bit further on, they noticed a row of Quonset huts that housed the reptiles. After a few more miles, they spotted a roadside sign announcing a "UFO Watch Tower' beside a small trailer and a windsock.

"I read somewhere that this valley has lots of UFO sightings," Lilly said in explanation.

They both agreed that all in all, the valley gave off some weird vibes.

The sky had grown overcast with the sun making brief, occasional cameo appearances. The low-hanging, gray curtain of clouds melded into the icy blue, snow- packed summits of the peaks. Soon it became apparent they were gaining altitude for the scrubby plain was giving way to knee-high prairie grass and foothills in the distance that appeared cloaked in pine. Several minutes later, they spotted a sign alerting them that Villa Grove, Elevation 7,986 feet, lay just ahead.

A half-dozen or so old-timey store fronts lined either side of the highway. It wasn't very difficult to spot The Villa Grove Trade as there seemed to be a scarcity of commercial establishments on the short strip of town. The sign on the false store front announced General Store Since 1882. The hand-painted lettering on the windows advertised art, espresso, burgers, pies, and Wi-Fi. They pulled up beside it and Soledad started to dismount.

"Wait," Lilly said, reaching behind the seat for her bag. She grabbed a manila envelope, withdrew something, and handed it to him. He could see it was a photograph.

"It's Kate," she said.

"A nice-looking girl," he said, studying it. "Do you think she still looks anything like this?"

Lilly seemed to think about this for a moment. "I kind of doubt it." She shook her head. "Not after being on the run. Let's go."

A bell chimed when they entered, but they didn't see anyone behind the counter. The few tables in the dining area also sat empty. Soledad leaned down and inspected a display case next to the counter that held an assortment of pies and pastries. They stood waiting for a minute before a woman emerged from what might have been a storeroom.

She was a thin, older woman with coarse features and hair the unnatural color of something from a bottle. She smiled at them and dropped a small cardboard box marked Slim Jims on the counter.

"Good morning, folks. Or is it afternoon already? So, what can I get you?" she asked with a broad smile.

Lilly wondered how many cigarettes it had taken to make that voice. She wore a plaid blouse that revealed her wrinkled décolletage and the top of a pack of cigarettes peeking from the top of her bra.

Lilly looked at Soledad who shrugged. "A couple of coffees and one of those apple and walnut bear claws would be great."

The woman started to turn around when Soledad said, "We're also wondering if you might be the person who called Hattie a few days back."

The woman's eyes narrowed as she digested the question for a moment before replying. "Are you cops?"

Soledad shook his head. "No. We're just looking for the young lady who left the message."

"We're her family," Lilly chimed in. "Her aunt and uncle. We've come to bring her home."

The woman merely nodded.

Lilly took the photograph from the envelope and held it out to her. "Is this her?"

The woman squinted at it for a long moment before answering. "Yeah, I think so. She looks a might different. Rougher around the edges, if you know what I mean."

"What can you tell us about her?" Lilly asked.

"Not much. She and her young man have come in here on maybe half a dozen occasions. Polite young man. A charmer. Always asks me how I'm doing, and even seems to mean it. He mostly just buys coffee, once or twice a couple of burgers. She comes in mostly just to use the restroom."

"Do you know how we can find them?"

"From what I gather they're working out on the Dalton place. Living out there in a trailer."

"And how can we find this Dalton guy?"

"Not a guy. A woman. Sunny Dalton. Of course, she has a ne'er-do-well son by the name of Caleb."

"Can you give us directions?"

"Sure. Get back on the highway and head north. Just a little way up you'll see a sign on the left that says Bonanza. It's an old, abandoned mining camp at the very end of the road. The Dalton Place is about four miles in on the right. You can't miss it. There's a big pile of rocks by the gate with a bronze elk on top."

"Did you notice what kind of vehicle they're driving?" Soledad asked.

"Some old Jap cars. A puke yellow color. I did notice it had Texas plates. Should I leave room for cream?" she asked, turning back to the coffee urns.

"Sure, thanks," Lilly said. "We appreciate the information."

"Is she in some kind of trouble?" the woman asked without turning around.

"I hope not," Lilly replied.

The woman handed them a couple of mugs. "I forgot to ask if you wanted these to go."

"No, this is fine," Soledad replied.

She reached into the display case, removed a bear claw, and placed it on a plate. "That'll be ten even."

As Soledad leafed through his wallet, she looked at Lilly. "Listen, I oughta warn you about some things," she said. "Hold on though. I've got another customer," she said as a tall, older man wearing a fringed, black leather jacket and a black Stetson came in and stepped up to the counter.

"Luther," the woman greeted him cheerfully. "You're all dolled up. It must be Friday. You need coffee?"

"Sure do," he replied as he eyed Lilly and Soledad.

"Aren't you leaving a little earlier than usual?" the woman asked.

"I'm hoping to get Annie to come up and spend the night. Maybe the weekend." He handed her a five. "Keep the change," he said as the woman handed him a coffee in a to-go cup.

"Here go, Luther. You drive safe and have a good one. Tell Annie to drop by and tell me about all the big city life I'm missing out on."

The man laughed. "Liz." He tipped his hat and walked out the door.

The woman watched him leave before turning back to Soledad and Lilly. "He's got a lady friend in Alamosa he drives down and sees every Friday."

"You were going to warn us about something." Lilly said when the woman stared at them absently.

"Oh, right. I wouldn't be talking out of school if I told you about Sunny Dalton. She's not what you'd call a beloved pillar of our community. She and that no account son of hers moved here maybe six years back. From Arizona, I'm told. What I heard was she paid cash for that ranch of hers. That got the ears buzzin' around here. Lots of speculation about where she mighta got that kind of money. Someone told me Dalton claimed it was inheritance money. But Gerta, our valley busy body, wasn't satisfied with that and started nosing around. She got on the internet and even went so far as to hire someone in Phoenix to look into them. It seems Sunny Dalton had been suspected of murdering her husband who was himself some kind of notorious drug dealer in those parts. Apparently, she was never charged. Next thing you know, she's up here."

She paused for a moment before going on.

"Now days, there's no telling what kind of nefarious shit she's up to, but I'm guessing it's not on the up and up. I'm just saying. I can tell you that Dalton's been trying to buy up every parcel of land around here that she can get her greedy hands on. That old gentleman who was just here. Luther Catanach. His family's been ranching in these parts for a hundred years. Sunny Dalton's been pressuring the old coot for a year now to sell out, but he won't budge. Least ways not to the likes of her, he says."

She paused to reach into her shirt and pull out her pack of cigarettes. She lit one with a Bic lighter that she also retrieved from the folds of her bosom, took a long drag and continued on.

"I'm only telling you this because you must be careful with your inquiries. Sonny Dalton's a paranoid, scheming hell bitch if you want my honest opinion."

Soledad pulled a face and looked at Lilly. "Well, we'll keep that in mind. Can you recommend any accommodations in your fair town?"

"Not much here. We usually rent out a couple of rooms out back, but they're currently occupied. You're probably better off going up to Salida. It's twenty-five miles or so up the highway on the other side of the pass."

"Thanks for the heads up about the Daltons," Soledad said. "It was Liz, right? Do you mind if we get some to-go cups?" He grabbed a napkin and wrapped up the bear claw.

"Sure thing. And let me top you off," Liz replied.

"So, what's the plan?" Lilly asked as they walked back to the truck.

"I have a feeling this is going to take more than a day. I say we first go and see the lay of the land and take it from there. I guess we could always drive into Salida and get a steak and a motel room."

"Did you find it curious that she asked us if we were cops?" Lilly asked, taking the bear claw from him.

"Maybe not so much in light of what she told us about the Daltons."

"How about what she said about Leroy Burns? You know, about him being this polite young man. Always asking her how she's doing. Could we be missing something?" She took a bite of the bear claw. "Eeee, this is good."

"You mean is it possible that Leroy Burns fell in with the wrong crowd, just got tempted by the wages of sin, and he's really an upstanding kind of a guy? It happens, doesn't it? I mean it could be that he and Kate are just a couple of kids in love and on the run. Like in some movie."

She handed him the other half of the bear claw. "She also said he was a charmer. I don't know, but in my book, that means he's probably a manipulative asshole."

"Ouch. Remind me to drop charming from the list of my qualities. So, let's go take a look and see the witch's lair," he said, shoving part of the bear claw into his mouth.

"I don't like where this is going," Lilly said after they had driven a couple of miles down the road to Bonanza. "I mean why in the hell couldn't Bonnie and Clyde have just shacked up in some motel in Kansas? Or pick some place to hide out that's warm. Cozumel would've been nice. Anywhere but an isolated place like this and living with a nest of vipers."

Soledad nodded. "Yeah, somewhere by the ocean would've been nice. We could be lazing around the beach while we nose around."

"It's been a while since I've been on a beach. I don't even own a bathing suit."

She thought of the last time she had worn one. Huatulco. It had been six, almost seven years ago. She and Estevan had spent a lost, lazy weekend there. Three months later, the Sinaloa cartel had killed him, and she had been forced to flee for her life.

"Maybe once this is over," Soledad said. "I know a guy who has a casita up the coast from Tulum. It's pretty isolated. We wouldn't have to leave. You wouldn't need a suit either." He looked at her and grinned.

"And what would Jeronimo say? I mean about the two of us. You're the Human Resources guy. Is there anything in his policy manual about employees fraternizing?"

"Hey, haven't you figured out yet that we're his golden children? We can do no wrong. He gives us all the choice assignments. Right?"

Lilly didn't reply, but instead watched the open countryside give way to pockets of forest. Soledad was right about them having favored status. Why else trust them with something like this? But she was determined to tell Jeronimo that she was done with this kind of work. She wanted a normal life; to be able to sleep at night; to not be afraid to travel somewhere and risk being recognized by someone from her past.

"Here it is," Soledad said, interrupting her thoughts. He pointed to a large metal gate flanked by an immense pile of pink granite boulders, atop of which stood a bronze statue of a bull elk. Beyond the gate they could see a rutted, muddy road leading into the forest, but they could see little else other than a quill of smoke rising from the tree line several hundred yards in. Soledad pulled in and stopped next to the intercom mounted on a metal pole.

"What do you think?" he asked. "Should we pay a call?"

"And what's our play? Normally I'd say the direct approach is best, but we don't know what we're really dealing with."

Her mind flashed back to El Paso and what the direct approach had almost cost she and Harlan. They could've waited that situation out also. And how many lives might've been spared if they had?

She shrugged. "I don't know what to think.".

"I'd say our best bet is to wait for them to leave and try to get them in a place where it's not likely to be confrontational. If she really wants out, that'll be in our favor."

"Wait them out, but for how long? I got the impression from the cashier that they don't go into town that often."

Soledad glanced in both directions. "Not a lot of cover for us to set up surveillance. We're going to need to come up with something. Like you said, the problem is that we don't know what we're dealing with. If Burns is hooked up with these Daltons in something illicit, it might make it complicated. I guess we could always sneak in and abduct her, but it might be risky since we don't know the layout."

"Then I guess we should wait and maybe we'll get lucky," Lilly replied.

He slipped the truck into reverse and started to back out just as a silver, late model Range Rover pulled in behind them.

"It looks like they might've forced our hand," he said, lifting his gaze to the rear-view mirror.

Lilly turned and looked behind them. She could see two people in the front seat. From what she could tell the driver was a woman although the hat the driver wore made it difficult to be sure.

"What do we do?" she asked.

Soledad thought for a moment. "Ad lib it, I guess. I've got a story I used once in Vera Cruz when I got caught snooping around someone's property. It's all I've got."

She glanced in the side mirror and saw a stocky, bearded man wearing jeans and a denim shirt dismount on the passenger side. She noticed he wore a holstered handgun on his belt. He seemed to give a quick glance at their license plate before coming up on Soledad's side. Soledad lowered his window.

"Good afternoon," Soledad said cordially.

The man didn't reply but instead leaned in and studied them, his gluey eyes reflecting nothing other than a dull scrutiny.

"Can I help you?" he said after a moment, his voice flat, without inflection, and like his eyes, without any sign of animation.

"Yeah," Soledad said. "My girlfriend and I were just cruising around and checking out the countryside. Is this your place?"

The man blinked slowly and seemed to consider the question for a moment. "Yeah, it is. If you're looking to buy property, it's not for sale."

"Would you maybe be interested in leasing part of it?"

"Leasing? For what?"

"Solar farm. You know, solar panels. We can pay top dollar. Or at least my uncle can. There wouldn't be any cost to you or work you'd have to do. You would just sit back and enjoy a guaranteed steady income."

He didn't say anything right away. Instead, he blinked slowly a couple of times and then glanced back at the Range Rover. "Hang on," he said, turned, and walked back to the driver's side window.

"What the hell, Jaime? You really think you can sell that story? I could've come up with something better than that."

"Such as? Look, I just want to see if we can get in there for a quick look see. We need to know where the trailer is. Could you tell the guy's loaded?" he added.

"What do you mean?"

"I mean he's high. You couldn't smell it? Here he comes," he said, nodding at the mirror.

"You have a business card?" the man asked.

"I sure don't. I'm just looking for my uncle as a favor. You can always call him though and he'll vouch for me. Like I said, this is easy money for a landowner."

The man they assumed might be Caleb Dalton seemed to think for a moment. "Okay, my mom's willing to give you fifteen minutes and no more. Follow us in," he said, and turned back to the Range Rover.

"And just who is he supposed to call? If they call your bluff, then what?"

He held up his finger and pulled out his cell phone and looked for the number. "I've got it covered," he said, punching a number and putting the phone on speaker. It rang several times before she answered.

"Mariposa. *¿Cómo está?* It's Jaime Soledad. I need a favor. This is your personal cell number, right?"

"*Si.* How can I be of assistance?"

"For the next two or three days whenever someone calls this number, I want you to answer Harris Solar Energy. If someone happens to ask for Frank Harris, you say he's out of the country and is unavailable. You are his personal secretary, and you will be happy to take a message. You got it? "They listened to her repeat his instructions. "Good. *Gracias,* Mariposa," he said and disconnected. "Just follow my lead," Soledad said as the gate swung open.

They pulled to the side to allow the Range Rover to pass. The road led into the tree line and after a short distance opened onto a clearing. An expansive, two-story log cabin-like dwelling sat atop a small knoll. Several outbuildings, one of which appeared to be a barn with an adjacent corral occupied a clearing a hundred yards or so from the house. Just beyond the barn, they saw a small house trailer.

"Bingo," Soledad said, nodding at the trailer.

He pulled up behind the Range Rover and they watched the Daltons dismount. Sunny Dalton was a petite, compact woman. She wore a full-length quilted jacket, riding boots, and a wide, flat-brimmed felt hat. She shot them a brief, dismissive glance and made her way to the porch.

She and Soledad got out and followed Caleb as he ushered them onto the porch and through the front door. The foyer's floors were pink, polished granite, the walls finished in a glassy, pale gold color. The only adornments were a mounted elk head and a large black and white framed photograph of a snow-capped mountain range.

Caleb held out his arm to motion for them to step into a side room where his mother sat enthroned behind a highly polished wooden desk the size of a pool table. She took off her hat and placed it carefully on the desk and smiled up at them.

Lilly had always placed a great deal of stock in first impressions and her initial take on Sunny Dalton was that she was what someone might label an alpha predator. The term black widow came to mind. Her eyes reflected a kind of cunning deliberation coupled with almost overt menace. They reminded her of her former bank robbing accomplice Gus Solomon's eyes. In other words, Sunny Dalton was a sociopath.

"Do you have identification?" Dalton asked, not bothering with introductions.

"Sure," Soledad said, pulling out his wallet, removing his driver's license, and placing it on the desk in front of her. "And who might I have the pleasure of addressing?"

She leaned over and studied his driver's license without picking it up. "Florida. You're a long way from home. How much are you offering per acre to lease?" she inquired in a husky voice.

"You'd have to talk to my uncle about that. I'm here on vacation and he just asked me to keep an eye out for possible locations for a solar farm. All I know is he would cover all the development costs. Like I told your son here, it's easy, steady, no fuss income."

She nodded and turned her gaze on Lilly, took her measure, and looked back at Soledad. "I'll give it some thought when I have less pressing matters. Can you leave me your uncle's number?" she asked, pushing a notepad and pen across the desk.

"Sure thing." He took out his phone, opened it up, and jotted Mariposa's number on the pad. "Harris Solar Energy. My uncle's name is Frank Harris. I wrote it down for you. He'll welcome a call. I guess we'll be on our way. I appreciate your time." He offered her a wide smile, took Lilly by the elbow, and led her back out into the foyer.

"You should take up conning old ladies out of their savings," she whispered. "But something tells me she didn't buy it."

"Yeah, she seems way too crafty. Let's just get out of here before she pounces."

They stepped out onto the porch and immediately spotted Caleb standing at the edge of the drive and speaking with a young, bearded man dressed in overalls. Gauging from their postures and Caleb's wild gesticulations, they looked like they were arguing.

"Leroy Burns," she said. "He looks different from his photo, but it's him."

"Yeah. He doesn't look anything like he did in Houston, but I agree. It's him alright."

They climbed into the truck, and Soledad backed up and stopped beside the two men before lowering his window.

"Thanks for the hospitality," Soledad said.

Caleb Dalton offered him a sullen stare and turned his attention back to Burns who studied them with a sort of wild-eyed intensity. Soledad raised his window and pulled away.

"Shit. This is beginning to seem like we stumbled on a bunch of psychos. Now what?" Lilly asked.

"We need to think about it. You have any ideas?"

"All I know is that woman is evil, everyone here seems unhinged or on drugs, and the sooner we get Kate away from here the better. I say we wait for dark, and we sneak in."

"I don't know," Soledad said. "For all we know they might have dogs or surveillance cameras. If we go knocking on the door of that trailer, we don't know what kind of situation we're walking into."

"I don't care. I say let's do this. We park a ways up the road and we walk through the woods. I go in by myself. It'll be less threatening that way. You can keep watch outside just in case I run into trouble. Look, I know her."

"You know her. Sure." He shook his head. "You only think you know her. But you don't know Leroy."

"I'm telling you, I can do this, Jaime."

"Okay. We'll do it your way. But mind you, I'm staying close. We'll do it soon as it gets dark."

He looked at this watch. "It's still early. How about we drive to Salida, get a steak, and we can still be back here by nightfall. If we can get her out of there tonight, I say we high tail it south. We can be in Santa Fe in time for breakfast."

"And then the border?"

"And then the border. We'll have Mariposa arrange for a plane and we can be in Mexico City by tomorrow night."

Lily nodded. It sounded too easy, but at least they had had a plan. "Okay. Let's get some food."

"You owe me a nice dinner," Lilly said as she tilted back the bottle of Negra Modelo.

It had taken a lot longer than expected to reach Salida due to a jack-knifed trailer home at the summit of the nine-thousand-foot-high pass above the town. A sudden flurry of light snow and sleet in the pass had rendered the highway treacherous. Consequently, it was five when they found themselves searching for a place to eat. They both decided they couldn't risk spending too much time in a restaurant if they hoped to be back at the Dalton place by nightfall. So here they sat in the Subway parking lot sharing a foot-long Italian sub and a six-pack of beer.

"I know this restaurant in Tulum'" Soledad said, pausing to swallow. "It's got the best seafood in the Yucatan. We could stop there on the way down the coast."

"I don't eat fish."

"Let me guess. You were raised Catholic, and you've had your fill of fish sticks."

"No. I was raised in the Church of Neglect and Grand Larceny. I guess Jeronimo didn't tell you, but he probably didn't know this anyway." She finished her beer and reached for another one. "We'll share," she said in response to his look of disapproval. "I spent four months in Alaska working on a salmon cannery boat. No more fish for me."

"I love it when you fill in the blanks on your past."

"How about if I told you I studied criminal justice for two semesters in community college? I was going to be a cop just like this asshole I was married to at the time."

He looked at her and shook his head. "You scare me sometimes."

"Only sometimes? You should be scared of me most of the time. Where are we going with this?" she said after a moment of silence.

"I told you. Once we have her, we get her across the border and let Jeronimo take it from there."

"No, I meant us. You and I."

He swallowed the remainder of his sandwich and looked at her. "Where do you want it to go?"

She paused to edit on the wall of her mind what she wanted to say. "You have to realize my life has been nothing but one long train wreck. I've been bouncing around from one fucked up situation to another. Men. Trouble with the law. Lots of bad choices. And then I end up working for Jeronimo and I think things could be different. And here we are dealing with this can of worms. I'm not worth a shit with relationships," she added.

When he didn't reply, she took a swallow of beer and went on. "I've been thinking. Jeronimo wants to make some legitimate investments in the States. I haven't wanted to travel here because I thought I might be on some watch list. But now I know that isn't a problem. I think I want to come back. I'm tired of looking over my shoulder whenever I'm traveling around Mexico. I'm going to ask Jeronimo if there's some work I could do for him somewhere in the States."

Soledad nodded. "That sounds like a good plan," he said and left it at that. He turned on the ignition and started to back up.

"Jaime. Wait," she said, reaching over and touching his arm. "About us. I don't know. It's been so long since I've let my guard down with anyone. Don't get me wrong. I like what we have so far. I just don't know where everything's going. I want to play it as it goes. A day at a time. Is that okay?"

"Sure. A day at a time. We better go," he said and pulled out of the lot.

Kate came out of the bedroom carrying the small duffle containing all her possessions. She glanced at Leroy who hadn't looked up from his game of solitaire. She held the bag at arm's length and then dropped it on the floor. Only then did he look up from the cards.

"Looks like you're going somewhere. If you want, I can call up the bellboy to help you with your bag,' he said with obvious sarcasm.

"I thought we weren't coming back here. You know, afterward. You said…."

"I know what I said." He glanced back down at his cards. "Yeah, we're leaving afterward."

She walked over to the table and sat down across from him. "I need to tell you something. Hey, look at me," she said when he laid down another card. He looked at her, his annoyance obvious.

"After this goes down, I'm leaving. On my own," she added. "Look, by morning they'll be looking for us. And I don't mean the cops."

"What do you mean?"

"You want to get the drop on them, tie them up, and then we take off with the money. Do you really think the ice queen is going to let us run? She and Caleb will come looking for us."

"Let 'em. They can't look everywhere."

"What I'm saying is we need to split up. Our chances are better. And you know that. You were the one that wanted to do that after we left Houston."

He didn't say anything, but instead simply stared at her.

"You go to Mexico by yourself. You can drop me off anywhere. Alamosa. Albuquerque. I don't care. I can catch a bus back to Houston. That means you and I…. We can't be together. Not anymore. I want a fresh start," she added when he didn't reply.

"Okay," he said after a moment. "But it doesn't change the way we're doing this. I've been thinking though. Instead of me getting the drop on them, you better carry the piece. You do it. They won't be expecting that. Then it's just like we talked about. We tie them up and leave them for someone to find in the morning. We just have to come back here, take the car and ditch it somewhere. We take their truck. I figure we can be a good way into New Mexico by the time they figure anything out. I can steal another car and we'll be in the clear."

"And you'll drop me off somewhere?"

He sighed. "Sure. I get it. I do."

"Look, Leroy. If I went with you to Mexico nothing would change. We'd always be looking over our shoulders. That's no way to live. Not the two of us together. I figure on my own I can disappear easier. You could, too."

He looked down at the cards and shrugged. "Did I ever tell you that my grandma raised me when my mom ran off with some car salesman? It was my grandma who taught me to play this," he said, tossing a card on the table. "Only she called it solitary. She explained that it was a game of chance. A game you play alone. Solitary was just like life, she told me. I guess she was right."

He reached down beside his chair and brought up a small backpack. "All my earthly belongings." He reached inside, withdrew a snub-nose revolver like the kind Kate had seen on television cop shows.

"Smith and Wesson 38 Special. I took it off this Korean guy we robbed once." He held it up for her to see before sliding the gun across the table. "Do you think you can carry this without your pants falling down?" he asked with a smirk.

She stared at the handgun for a few seconds before picking it up. She had never held a gun before.

"And what in God's name am I supposed to do with this?"

"You point at them. They see that pistol and they won't do anything stupid. You just have to do it before either of them makes a move."

"I don't know about this, Leroy. I don't know anything about guns. I've never fired one."

He took the revolver from her and held it up. "You just have to cock it like this," he said, pulling back the hammer. "Then you're in business. I guarantee you, when they hear that hammer cock, they'll freeze. Caleb's balls will rise up in his throat. You just got to keep this somewhere you can get to it quickly. It'll fit in the pocket of your jacket. Just keep your hands in your pockets so they can't see you're carrying it." He handed it back to her. "Try it in your pocket."

She started to take it from him when there was a knock on the door. Leroy looked at this watch.

"That asshole's early. He said eight. Quick, stick it in your jacket."

She got up, grabbed her jacket, and tried to slip the handgun into her pocket. "It's not going to fit." she said.

"Shit! Give it here." He grabbed the gun from her and stuck it in the back waistband of his jeans. "Be cool," he said and turned and opened the door.

"Can I help you?" Kate heard him say.

She moved up behind Leroy and saw a woman wearing a down jacket and a watch cap standing on the stoop.

"Hattie sent me," the woman said, peering at Kate over Leroy's shoulder. "Mind if I come in?"

28

Leroy turned and looked at Kate. "What the fuck?"

Lilly stepped through the doorway before he could stop her. "Calm down, Leroy. Let me explain," Lilly said.

"How in the hell do you know my name? Shit, Kate. What did you do?"

Lilly brushed past him and looked at Kate who appeared just as confused and surprised as Leroy. The woman at the diner was right, Lilly thought. Kate bore only a passing resemblance to her photo. Her hair was longer and badly needed a shampoo and a cut. Without makeup, she appeared older, and as the woman had said, rough around the edges.

Lilly shot a quick glance at Leroy. He also looked haggard. Unlike his last mug shot, he also had longer hair, a beard, and was missing his smug smile. They both wore what looked like grubby, Goodwill hand me downs.

Her mind flashed back to the days when she lived on the streets of Houston. At one time, she found herself down to one dress, and the only cosmetics and toiletries she had were the ones she managed to shoplift.

"I know this is all pretty sudden, but… Look, it's your move, Kate. You said you wanted to come home."

Leroy grabbed Kate by the arm and swung her around. "What are you doing?"

"Let her go," Lilly said. "I said let her go," she said again when Leroy yanked Kate toward him.

He turned on Lilly. "You need to get the fuck out of here."

"Stop it! I called Hattie," Kate yelled.

"You did what?" He looked at Kate. "We can't be doing this shit now."

"I had the woman at the trading post call. I didn't think anyone would show up this soon."

Leroy pulled the Smith and Wesson out of his waistband and pointed it at Lilly. "Get out! Now!"

"You won't shoot me, so you might as well put it down."

"Oh, yeah?"

"I've had a lot scarier people than you point a gun at me. I know when to worry. You don't worry me, Leroy."

He cocked the revolver and pointed the barrel directly in her face, inches from her nose. Lilly shook her head and smiled. Leroy lowered the gun.

"Shit!" He looked at Kate. "You're fucking this up."

"What exactly is she fucking up?" Lilly asked.

"We're supposed to…"

"Shut up, Kate," he said, his eyes still on Lilly.

"Look, if you're worried about cops. We're not cops. And we didn't tell anyone where you are. We just want to take Kate back."

"Who's we?"

"It doesn't matter. We just want to take her with us and then we'll be gone. No questions asked. No harm done."

"Leroy," Kate said, taking his arm. "Let me go."

Leroy looked at her for a long moment before sticking the .38 back in his waistband. "You should have told me," He said, turning away and dropping on the sagging sofa in obvious disgust.

"I did. You weren't listening."

"And what am I supposed to tell them? You know what'll happen if we just walk away? I need you, Kate." He dropped his face in his hands. "It's all going to shit."

Lilly looked at Kate. "Look, I don't know what's happening here, but if you ask me, it sounds like something you shouldn't be a part of."

Kate looked at both in turn before going and sitting beside Leroy. "It's not too late for both of us to leave," she said, taking his hand.

Leroy shook his head. "I can't. Not without some kind of score. Did you forget there are cops in four states looking for us? I can't run without money. Not anymore."

"You have to choose, Kate," Lilly said, filling the silence that followed. "Do you understand what I'm saying?"

There was suddenly the rumbling sound of a vehicle pulling up outside. Leroy jumped to his feet, hurried to the window, and pulled aside the blanket that served as a makeshift curtain.

"It's them. Goddammit!" He looked at Kate and then at Lilly. "You! Get in the bedroom and keep your mouth shut."

"We can put an end to this right now," Lilly said. "Tell the Daltons whatever you need to, and Kate and I leave."

"No, we can't." He looked again at Kate. "Are you gonna do this or not?"

Kate looked up at Lilly. "Wait for me. We'll be back. I promise. Then I'll go with you."

"You're making a mistake."

"Shut up and get in the bedroom," Leroy hissed.

Lilly hesitated. She could pull the Glock from her waistband and settle it now. She realized that within a few seconds it might be too late, and it could all go to hell. Caleb Dalton would recognize her. He would be armed. Leroy still had his gun. There was no guarantee what would happen. She couldn't take the chance of Kate getting caught in any crossfire.

She thought of Soledad waiting outside and wondered how he would react when he saw Dalton leave with Kate and Leroy. The only thing she could do was to wait in the bedroom and see if she might perhaps overhear what it was they were planning on doing.

"Okay. I'll wait for you," she said, and walked into the bedroom, closing the door behind her. A few seconds later, she heard a click. She tried to turn the doorknob and realized it was locked. Lilly pressed her ear to the door and tried to hear what was being said.

S oledad rose up from behind the propane tank where he had been hiding and stomped his feet to get some feeling back. He regretted not bringing something other than his leather work boots. The boots were soaked from the snow they had trudged through as they had made their way through the woods to the rear of the trailer.

It had been five minutes, maybe ten, since Lilly had entered the trailer. They had agreed on no more than fifteen minutes before Soledad hit the panic button and interceded. Regardless, he felt he needed to know what was happening inside.

He moved up to a jalousie window on the side of the trailer. Because of the three-foot-high cinder block foundation the trailer sat upon, it was difficult to put his ear to the window. The blanket blocking the window along with the loud hum of a generator in the woods behind the trailer made it next to impossible for him to make out anything that was being said. He heard Burns' voice, and then Lilly's, but both were shouting something unintelligible.

He contemplated walking up to the stoop to see if it might be easier to overhear their conversation from there. Then he heard Burns yell something that sounded like 'Get out now!' followed by Lilly's incomprehensible response.

Five more minutes and no more, he decided. In the meantime, he decided to move up beside the front door and be ready. Just as he began to round the corner of the trailer, he heard a vehicle approaching. He pulled back, and to his dismay, he recognized Dalton's Range Rover as it pulled to a stop in front. A moment later, he heard yelling coming from inside the trailer, but he still couldn't make out what was being said.

Whatever was happening, he had no choice now but to hope Lilly could deal with the situation. He pulled his Glock, peered around the corner, and saw the dome light inside the SUV come on as Caleb Dalton climbed out of the passenger side. Before the light went off, he saw Sunny Dalton in the driver's seat. What was going on, he wondered as he watched Dalton walk up to the door. He knocked, the door opened, and Dalton stepped inside.

"Are you two ready?" Lilly overheard Caleb Dalton ask.

"You're early," Leroy replied. "You said eight."

"No sense waiting. Catanach left for Alamosa hours ago. We go in there now and do it and you'll have a good head start long before he gets back."

She heard Kate say something she couldn't make out.

"Don't worry about that. It'll be a piece of cake. And we told you no one's gonna get hurt."

It suddenly grew quiet. Had Dalton grown suspicious about something? Lilly gripped the Glock and stepped back from the door and waited, but there was only silence.

She couldn't allow Kate to go through with whatever it was the Daltons had planned. Her only choice seemed to be to take her chances and end this now. She stepped back, raised her leg and was about to kick the door when she heard Kate say she would be right behind them, and that she had to pee first. A couple of seconds later, Lilly heard the front door of the trailer slam shut. Lilly put her head against the door and listened.

"Kate," she said softly. "Are you there?"

"What's your name?" Kate asked. It sounded as if she too had her head pressed to the door.

"I'm Lilly. Listen to me. Just tell them you're not going. It's not right what you're doing. It's stupid and dangerous."

"I can't. I'll be back. I promise."

"Kate. Kate!"

A few seconds later, Lilly heard the front door close.

"Shit, Shit!" She kicked at the door in frustration.

L illy kicked the door knob a couple of more times, but it didn't budge. She was about to shoot it off when she heard the front door open.

"Lilly!" Soledad said quietly.

"In here. Unlock the door."

A second later, Soledad unlocked the door. "What happened?"

"We need to go," she said, turning for the front door.

"Hold on," he said, pulling her back. "They stopped down at the house. What are they doing?"

"I'll tell you what they're doing. They're planning on robbing somebody."

She suddenly remembered the name Dalton had mentioned. "Wait. I think I know who they're robbing. Catanach. Wasn't that the name of the old man who came into the diner when we were there? I think that's who they're planning to rob. It sounded like they're expecting him to be in Alamosa."

"And I seem to recall the old guy saying he was coming back this evening with his lady friend. There's something else. Caleb's not alone. It looks like his mother's with him."

"We have to go."

"Go where? It'll take us ten minutes to get back to the truck. Bu then they'll likely be gone. And we don't have any idea where this Catanach even lives."

Lilly thought of something. "Liz. The woman at the diner. The cashier. She'll know. But we better hurry."

32

Sunny Dalton pulled up in front of their house. "You two sit tight. "We forgot some things," Caleb said as he and his mother both climbed out and disappeared inside.

Neither of them said anything for a moment. "I don't want to do this," Kate said finally.

Leroy didn't reply, but instead rocked back and forth ever so slightly. Kate could tell he was nervous.

"They're gonna double cross us for sure," Leroy said. "Here," he said, pulling the revolver from the back of his waistband and handing it to her. "Take this."

"I told you. I'm not carrying a gun."

"You have to. It'll be the only way. Like I told you, they won't expect you to be carrying. If you see things going sideways, you pull it. That's all you have to do. I'll take it from there."

She hesitated for a moment and then took the gun and with some difficulty stuffed it into the pocket of her jacket.

"I'm not shooting anybody. You hear me?"

"Don't worry. You won't have to."

They sat in silence for another couple of minutes before they saw the Daltons step out onto the porch. It looked like Caleb was carrying a sledgehammer and what appeared to be a long crowbar.

"Shit,' Leroy said. "She's carrying. They both are."

"Are you sure?"

"Yeah, I'm sure. I can see her holster. His, too."

"Come on, Leroy. Please. We can stop this now."

Leroy didn't reply, but instead simply stared straight ahead. Kate started to pull the revolver from her jacket, but Leroy grabbed her arm to stop her.

"Wait!" he hissed. "Let's wait and give it a chance."

Before Kate could say anything, the Daltons both climbed in. No one said anything until they reached the gate.

"It'll be quick and dirty," Caleb muttered. "We'll be in and out in less than an hour. You can bank on it."

"Maybe even less if we find that suitcase right away," Sunny Dalton added, tilting her head to glance back at them in the rear-view mirror, but Kate couldn't make out her eyes. "Then you two love birds can high tail it to Mexico."

Kate glanced at Leroy who had again started to rock ever so slightly back and forth. My kharma, she thought. Nothing was going to change the course they were on. Just like Leroy said, just wait it out. She dropped her head back and closed her eyes.

The drive to Catanach's ranch took no more than five or ten minutes. The gate was closed and appeared to be secured with a heavy padlock. Caleb slipped on a pair of work gloves and retrieved the sledgehammer from the floorboard before climbing out and walking up to the gate. It took a couple of blows to break open the lock.

No one said anything as they drove for a quarter mile up a winding dirt road that led through dense stands of pine. The trees suddenly gave way to a large clearing where a two-story house stood in the center. Other than a couple of lighted windows on the first floor, the house appeared dark.

Sunny Dalton pulled up in front of the small yard and cut the ignition. They sat there a moment in silence, the only sound was the ticking of the hot engine.

"Just like I told you," Caleb said. "No dogs. And his truck's gone. Let's go."

He dismounted, crowbar in hand, and waited for the others to get out. After a moment's hesitation, Leroy climbed out and before he could take a step, Caleb grabbed his arm.

"Hold on," Caleb said, placing the crowbar on the hood. "Arms up. Come on," he said when Leroy looked at him in confusion. "I need to know you're not carrying. It's a trust thing."

Leroy glanced back at Kate who still sat in the back seat. "And I'm supposed to trust you," he said, lifting his arms.

"That's just the way it works," he replied, quickly frisking Leroy. "He's clean, Mom."

Only then did Sunny Dalton climb out from behind the wheel. "Okay, kids," she said. "Let's get to it."

Kate climbed out and shot a quick glance at Leroy who nodded. Caleb ignored her and followed his mother to the house.

"What do we do?" she whispered to Leroy as they followed them in.

"Give me the gun."

"What are you going to do?"

"Give it to me. Hurry."

She fumbled with the gun but couldn't get it out of her pocket.

Caleb stopped and turned to look at them. "Come on. Get a move on."

Leroy shook his head in frustration. Caleb waited and fell in behind them. Kharma, she thought again. There was nothing to be done. She reached for Leroy's hand and followed him inside.

"**D**ammit," Soledad muttered as they pulled up to the Villa Grove Trade. A large neon sign in the window flashed the word 'Closed'.

"Now what do we do?" Lilly asked.

"Hold on. I think I see someone inside."

They both got out and walked up to the door. Sure enough, Liz stood behind the counter. It appeared as if she was counting her receipts. Soledad knocked and she looked up as if startled. It took a moment before she recognized them. She walked slowly to the door and opened it.

"I know you're closed, but we need your help," Soledad said.

"You guys get lost?" she asked, the caution in her voice obvious.

"No. We need to know how to get to Luther Catanach's place. Wasn't that his name? The old guy who was in here earlier?"

She shot him a questioning look "Why in God's name do you need to know that?"

"Look," Lilly cut in. "We think Sunny Dalton and her son are going to burglarize his house. And they think he's in Alamosa. Correct me if I'm wrong but didn't he say he was coming back this evening?"

"I don't get it. How do you know the Daltons are planning on doing such a thing?"

"It's not important how we know, but we need to get there and stop it."

"Does this have something to do with that young gal you're looking for?"

"Yeah, it does. We want to get her out of there."

"My God, for all I know there's a good chance Luther's already back by now. Best we call the sheriff." She pulled a cell phone from the pocket of her jacket.

"No cops," Soledad said, gently taking the phone from her. "Not yet. We can't get her involved with the law."

"You need to show us how to get there," Lilly said. "Please. If Catanach is there, it could get bad."

"The sheriff could put a stop to it."

"Look, Liz," Lilly said. "There's no time. You have to trust us on this. No law enforcement until we get her out."

"Are you guys really her aunt and uncle?"

"Not exactly. Please, just tell us how to get there."

Liz studied them for a moment. "Okay, but I'd have to show you. His gate ain't marked very well. Just let me lock up.

To their consternation, Liz moved at a leisurely pace, and it took almost five minutes for her to lock the cash register, turn off the lights, find her keys, and lock the front door.

"His ranch is on Bonanza Road. Just before the Dalton's place," Liz said, slipping in between them.

Fortunately, it took no more than a minute to reach the cut off to Bonanza. As they approached the turnoff, Soledad slowed because another vehicle with its blinker on was waiting to make the same turn. It was waiting to allow a long caravan of RVs coming from the opposite direction to pass by.

"Hey, that's Luther's pickup," Liz said. "You need to stop him."

Before Soledad could do anything, Luther quickly shot in between a couple of oncoming RVs, and Soledad was forced to wait for a break in the traffic before gunning it to catch up with Catanach. By then, the old man's taillights showed he was a good way up the road.

"You'd best hurry and catch him," Liz said. "His turn off is just up the road."

Soledad gunned it and caught up with Catanach's truck just as it pulled onto a side road. He pulled in behind Catanach as he slowed to a stop at the open gate. Their headlights showed Catanach and a woman in the passenger seat turning to look back at them.

"You'd better let me talk to him," Liz said.

As Lilly got out to allow Liz to dismount, she saw Catanach reach for the rifle in the rear window rack before climbing out of the cab.

"Luther," Liz yelled. "Hold on. It's me. Liz."

Catanach lowered his rifle. "Liz? What the hell's going on?"

"It's that bitch Sunny Dalton. She and Caleb are fixing to rob you."

"Rob me?" Catanach shook his head in confusion. "My gate's busted open. It's them?"

"Mr. Catanach," Lilly said, stepping up beside Liz. "Let me explain."

"Who are you?" he said, again raising his rifle.

"My name is Lilly. The Dalton's took a friend of ours. We're just trying to get her out of there before things go bad."

"I'm calling the sheriff," Luther said, turning to reach inside the truck.

"Hold on," Lilly heard Soledad yell from behind her. He stepped up to join the two women. "Tell him, Liz. Our friend left a message with you to call us and come get her."

"That's right, Luther. She did leave me a message saying she wanted to come home. She's been staying up at the Dalton's trailer. She and her boyfriend. This young gal is most likely caught up in this against her will," Liz offered.

Catanach appeared to consider this for a moment. "And you trust these people?"

Liz cast a glance at Lilly. "Yeah, I do."

"And you say the Dalton's plan on robbing me?"

"Yes sir," Soledad said. "And they're probably already up at your house. They thought you'd be in Alamosa. Look, Mr. Catanach. We're just asking for you to let us go in and get our friend out. Give us thirty minutes. If we're not out by then, you can call the sheriff."

"Jaime," Lilly whispered, her eyes still on Catanach. "That's crazy. Thirty minutes? Say the cops come and we don't make it out by then. Then what?"

Catanach appeared to consider Soledad's offer.

"All right. There's a deputy in the village who can get here right quick. You've got thirty minutes before I call in the law."

"Fair enough. Let's go," Soledad said, turning to Lilly.

They quickly scrambled back into the pickup. Soledad edged the pickup around Catanach's truck and started up the road.

"Tell me you've got some kind of plain in mind," Lilly said. "Jaime," she said when he made no effort to reply.

"We get the drop on them," he said finally.

"That's your plan?"

"If you have a better idea, I'm open to hearing it."

The road led up a hill and through thick forest for a short distance. Up ahead, they suddenly saw what they thought were lights from the house.

"I don't think we can risk driving any closer," Soledad said, quickly switching off the headlights. He cut the ignition, and they got out and carefully closed the doors. Soledad reached into the back of the pickup's bed, opened the storage locker, and began rummaging. He handed Lilly the two Kevlar vests.

"Really?" she asked.

"Put it on. Better safe than sorry."

Next, he retrieved the two Glocks, a flashlight, and finally the shotgun. He handed her a couple of magazines for the Glocks. He slipped on his Kevlar vest and slammed one of the magazines into his Glock before shoving it into his waist band. Reaching back again to the locker, he pulled out a box of shotgun shells. He broke open the box of shells on the side of the locker and stuffed a handful into the pocket of his jacket. He turned on the flashlight and shined it on his watch.

"Clock's ticking. We've got twenty-three minutes we have to hustle." he said and set off at a trot with Lilly close behind.

Sunny Dalton had already slipped inside and turned on a light in the entry hall by the time Leroy, Kate and Caleb reached the front door. The rows of mounted deer and elk heads lining the walls momentarily gave Kate pause. The heads along with the full-length mirror at the end of the hall lent a morbid surrealism to the dimly lit hallway.

They followed Sunny Dalton to the rear of the house and into a large, open kitchen. Just as Caleb had said, it seemed Luther Catanach hadn't spent a dime of his money updating the house, for the appliances appeared to date back to the fifties. A matching and faded avocado-colored oven and refrigerator sat on either side of badly chipped and stained porcelain sink. The floor was covered with dingy, faded linoleum except for a slightly tattered Navajo rug upon which sat a heavy, round wooden table, its surface bare except for a bottle of red wine, a vase of calla lilies, and a stack of newspapers.

Sunny Dalton eyed the table for a moment before sweeping the table's contents to the floor with her arm. The vase shattered as it hit the floor, scattering the lilies.

"Help me move the table," she barked.

Leroy hesitated before joining Caleb in sliding the heavy table to the side. Caleb grabbed the rug and flung it to the side. The linoleum beneath it appeared undisturbed.

"Are you sure that Mex woman you were screwing knew what she was talking about?" Sunny asked, shooting her son a look of annoyance.

Caleb quickly looked away as if he had been slapped. "I swear she said he kept his money under the table."

Sunny Dalton sighed and looked around the kitchen. "Search the place. Every fucking cabinet and closet. Tear up the carpet. Find it!" she screamed. "You," she said, pointing at Kate. "Come with me."

Kate followed Dalton as she checked an adjoining mud room before walking back through the kitchen and into a small adjoining room that contained a desk and stacks of boxes. Its floor also was covered with linoleum. Kate noticed a rifle sitting in the corner beside the desk, but before she could even consider reaching for it, Dalton nodded with her head for Kate to follow her.

The next room appeared to be a rarely used dining room gauging from the room's musty smell and the large mahogany-colored table heaped high with newspapers, magazines, and manila file folders. A large dusty China cabinet took up most of one wall. Beneath the table and covering most of the linoleum flooring was an eight by ten-foot length of soiled shag carpeting. Dalton leaned down to inspect the carpet, lifting one corner to see what might lie beneath it.

"Caleb! You all get in here." she yelled as she began frantically sweeping the table's contents to the floor. "Don't just stand there you stupid cow," she said to Kate. "Help me move this table."

It took all of Kate's reserve to keep from pulling the revolver out of her pocket and shooting Sunny Dalton where she stood. She would wait, she decided. Like Leroy said, wait until we see if the suitcase of money even existed. As she grabbed the end of the table, the revolver clunked loudly against the edge, but Dalton seemed not to notice.

Caleb hurried into the dining room carrying the crowbar with Leroy close behind. They both helped pull the table aside, and once it was clear, Caleb dragged the length of carpet away, exposing a small sheet of bare plywood. Caleb looked up at his mother and grinned.

"I told you we'd find it," he crowed and began to frantically pry up the plywood with the crowbar.

It took only a matter of a few seconds to loosen one end. He tossed the crowbar aside, and grasping the end of the plywood, yanked it free. An old, battered Samsonite suitcase lie cradled beneath it.

Caleb lifted it out, unsnapped the lid and opened it. Inside were neatly stacked bundles of money. Sunny Dalton made no effort to step closer to inspect the contents even as Caleb began greedily scooping up the bundles in both hands.

Leroy dropped to his knees beside him and gave a quick glance up at Kate. Now, he seemed to mouth. Sunny pulled her eyes away from the two men and looked at Kate.

"Caleb," she said calmly. "Get your nose out of there and come here."

"Goddammit, Kate!" Leroy hissed. "What are you waiting for?"

Kate reached into her pocket, her fingers grasping the butt of the revolver, but before she could pull it free, Sunny Dalton tugged a handgun from the folds of her long-quilted jacket and casually pointed it at Kate.

"Wait, wait," Leroy said, nervously. "What's going on?"

"It's show time, kids," Sunny said. She reached calmly into the pocket of her shirt and removed a joint. She produced a lighter from her coat pocket and lighted the joint, still pointing her gun at Kate.

"You two didn't really think we needed you. Well, we do. You see, it turns out you two are going to disappear. Just not like you thought. Come morning, old man Catanach is going to report he's been robbed. By then I'll have already called the sheriff to report our Range Rover is missing. And we'll tell him that we think you two must've stolen it. The cops will find it abandoned and out of gas on the road to Alamosa. And you two will be in the wind. Fugitives from the law. The thing is, they'll never find you. We'll make sure of that."

She pulled a roll of duct tape from her pocket and handed it to Caleb. "You two are dumber than I thought," she said as Caleb moved towards Leroy who still knelt beside the open suitcase.

"Get up and turn around," Caleb said, tearing off a length of the duct tape.

Leroy appeared to hesitate for a moment before getting to his feet. Caleb didn't see the crowbar in Leroy's hand until it was too late. Leroy swung the bar, striking Caleb a glancing blow on the side of his head.

The two began grappling with each other. Caleb attempted to pull his gun from its holster with one hand while struggling to free the crowbar from Leroy's grasp with the other. Somehow the gun came free and clattered to the floor. Both men fell to their knees and scrambled to recover it.

"Caleb! Get the fuck out of the way!" his mother yelled, turning her gun on them.

As the two men fumbled for the gun, Sunny Dalton fired, but the round smashed harmlessly into the wall behind the two men.

"Shoot him, Mom!" Caleb screamed.

"Move out of the way, god damn it!" she yelled as she took a step toward the two men.

Kate yanked the gun free from her pocket.

"Stop!" she screamed as she cocked the revolver and aimed it at Sunny Dalton.

Dalton swung around, turning her gun on Kate.

Lilly found it difficult to keep up with Soledad. The night was pitch black, the thin rind of moon rising over the mountains intermittently obscured by the cloud cover. The lights coming from the house at the end of the road provided the only directional beacon.

The deeply rutted, uneven road made it even more difficult. The ridges of dried mud felt like concrete, and she suddenly tripped and landed on all fours into a pothole filled with cold water. Fortunately, she managed to avoid dropping her Glock. She grimaced as she straightened. A flash of pain coursed down the length of her left thigh.

"Are you okay?" Soledad said, stopping to look back at her.

"I'm okay. Go." I'll catch up with you, she replied, pushing to her feet. She paused to catch her breath, took a gulp of the cold night air, and started again after Soledad.

When she finally caught up with Soledad, he was leaning against the Dalton's Range Rover and feeding shells into the shotgun. They were both breathing heavily.

"Damn you." She bent over with her hands on her thighs. "You should've asked Catanach for forty-five minutes."

"You ready?" he asked, still panting.

She nodded.

"Stay here and cover the front door. I'll go around back."

"I'll go through the front," she said as she started to walk toward the porch.

"No. You wait. You hear me? Cover the front," he said and slipped into the darkness around the corner of the house.

She stood there another moment, steadying herself before moving toward the porch and the open front door. It was then she heard the yelling coming from inside, followed by a single gunshot. She decided not to wait for Soledad. She raised the Glock and ran to the doorway.

37

Caleb lunged again for his gun that lay on the floor just out of his reach, but Leroy clawed him back.

"Shoot her!" Caleb yelled again as he swung at Leroy who clung to his legs.

The two women stood there staring at each other across the table, their guns pointed at each other. The gun felt heavier than Kate remembered, and she struggled to hold it steady in her trembling hands.

"Drop the gun, Dalton!"

Kate turned her head and saw the woman who had called herself Lilly standing in the doorway and pointing a handgun at Dalton.

Dalton appeared startled, and took a step back, shifting her gaze back and forth between Kate and Lilly.

"What the… fuck?!" she muttered loudly.

"I said drop it!"

"I'll shoot her," Dalton said. "I swear it." HHer voice betrayed a hint of uncertainty.

"You do and it'll be the last thing you ever do," Lilly said evenly.

Kate struggled to hold her gun steady but her hands were shaking so much that she could barely keep it pointed straight.

Dalton looked at.Lilly and seemed to smile. "So be it," Dalton said and fired.

Kate felt a hot, stinging sensation on her left shoulder. She flinched and squeezed the trigger. The boom of the three gunshots came in such close unison they sounded as one. Sunny Dalton tumbled back against the China cabinet, sending dishes and a box of silverware crashing onto the floor.

No one reacted for what seemed an eternity. Caleb again struggled frantically to break free from Leroy's grasp, but Leroy grabbed him by his belt and dragged him back. Caleb seemed to be screaming but Kate couldn't hear r him above the ringing in her ears.

Kate felt a hand trying to push her arms down. "Give me the gun," she thought she heard a voice say. "Kate. Let go," the voice said.

She turned her head and saw the Lilly woman standing at her side.

"It's okay," Lilly said, prying the gun from her grasp.

It was only then that Kate saw a blonde-haired man dressed entirely in black and carrying a shotgun leaning over Sunny Dalton. Dalton attempted to raise her gun, but the man pushed her arm down with his foot and held it there.

"Is she alright?" Kate thought she heard the man ask, for she still had difficulty hearing.

The Lilly woman nodded.

The blonde man fished a linen napkin from the scattered debris on the floor before leaning down and carefully removing the gun from Dalton's grasp. Then he walked over, and using the napkin, picked up Caleb's gun from the floor.

"Okay, here's what going to happen," Kate thought she heard the man say.

"Okay, here's what's going to happen," Soledad said, glancing down at the two men on the floor. "Leroy, take this tape and do Caleb's hands and feet," he said, kicking the roll of duct tape across to him. "Hurry it up. We don't have much time."

Lilly walked over to Sunny Dalton who was groaning and writhing in pain. The right shoulder of Dalton's shirt was soaked in blood. She attempted to sit up, but Lilly shoved her back. Dalton glanced up at Lilly, her eyes reflecting at first confusion that quickly morphed into a malevolent glare.

"Bitch," Dalton muttered weakly. She looked pale and there were beads of sweat on her forehead.

"You're lucky," Lilly said. "My aim was off."

Lilly reached over and retrieved another napkin from the floor. She stuffed it roughly into Dalton's shirt and then grabbed Dalton's hand and pressed it firmly against the wound, causing Dalton to shriek in pain.

"Best you hold it tight and don't let go or you'll bleed out," Lilly said, turning to look at Soledad. "How much time do we have?"

Soledad glanced at his watch. "Ten, maybe twelve minutes.

He handed Lilly the shotgun and picked up a plastic shopping bag from the dining room table and deposited the two handguns into it. He then went over and knelt beside the suitcase and began scooping up the loose bundles of money and stuffing it back into the suitcase.

Lilly went over to Kate who sat slumped over in a chair. "Are you okay?" Lilly asked, inspecting the rip in the sleeve of Kate's jacket. "You got hit," she said, inspecting the blood on her fingers. "It mustn't be too bad though. Not much blood."

When Kate didn't reply, Lilly squatted in front of her.

"Congratulations. You survived your second gun fight. Let's hope it's your last. We have to go. So, get it together. Do you understand?"

Kate looked at her and nodded. Lilly helped her to her feet and turned to Soledad. "Are we ready?"

"I'll get the truck. Meet me outside," he said, taking the shotgun from her and handing her the suitcase and the bag of guns. Then he hurried out of the room.

"You're just gonna leave us?" Caleb whimpered. "You shot my Mom, you bitch! She's hurt bad."

Lilly went over to him and picked up the roll of tape. "The cops and an ambulance will be here soon enough," she said, tearing off a piece of tape and pressing it over Caleb's mouth.

"What do you mean cops?" Leroy asked, his voice betraying his panic.

"Let's go," Lilly said. "Or would you like me to tape you up and leave you here with them?"

"That's our money," he replied, his voice breaking.

"Not anymore," she said, taking Kate by the arm and waving the gun at Leroy. "Now let's go," she said, guiding them both out the door.

Soledad ordered Leroy to get in the pickup's bed and keep his mouth shut or Soledad would leave him behind. They had Kate sit between them. She hadn't said anything since walking out of the house, and only then, a simple mutter of thanks.

Soledad drove down the rough road as fast as he dared. Halfway down, Lilly told him to stop.

"Why? We're cutting it close,"" he said, slowing.

"It'll just take a minute." She lifted the suitcase from behind the seat, opened it, and removed a roll of bills. "Come on," she said, taking Kate by the arm.

"What are you doing?" Soledad asked.

Lilly didn't reply. Once she and Kate were outside, she led Kate a short distance away from the truck and turned to her.

"Look, I don't know anything about the two of you. How you feel about Leroy. But it's time you two said your goodbyes." She turned away and walked over to the pickup.

"Get out, Leroy."

Leroy hesitated before clambering from the bed.

"What are you gonna do?" he asked, nervously.

"Here," Lilly said, handing him the roll of bills. "I'm guessing it can't be more than a mile or so through the woods to the Dalton's place. You get in your car and go. Understand? You run is what you do." She turned and climbed back inside the truck.

"You know that in about two minutes Catanach's going to call the sheriff?" Soledad said.

"Give it a minute," she replied.

Sure enough, a minute later Kate opened the door and hopped in beside Lilly. No one said anything as Soledad gunned the truck down the road.

Catanach had pulled his truck sideways, blocking any exit from the gate. Liz and Catanach's lady friend were nowhere to be seen. Soledad pulled to a stop.

"Bring the suitcase," he told Lilly.

They left Kate in the truck and walked up to Catanach who stood on the other side of his truck, his rife resting on the hood.

"Where are the women?" Soledad asked, stopping across the hood from him.

"I had them retreat to those trees across the road. In case there was gonna be any gunplay. I heard the shots," he added. "Anyone hurt?"

"Sunny's got a shoulder wound. You should have the sheriff call EMS."

Lilly joined Soledad and placed the plastic shopping bagck containing the guns on the hood before slinging the suitcase up next to the bag. "I'm sorry, but we left your house in a bit of a mess," she said.

Catanach leaned over the bag and peered inside.

"Their guns," Soledad explained.

Catanach grunted and then placed his hand on the suitcase. He gave it a slight heft but made no effort to open it.

"I'm not gonna ask what this was all about, but I'm guessing you got the girl," he said, nodding at their truck.

"She must mean something to you. To go to all this trouble, I mean." He paused a few seconds before continuing on. "I had a daughter once. She was a bit wild. Like her mother was at that age," he said with the suggestion of a smile. "She ended up giving my wife and I a lot of grief." He paused and seemed to take a deep breath. "I did something crazy like this once. Trying to pull her ass from the coals."

"And did you? Pull her ass from the coals?" Lilly asked, filling the silence that followed.

"For a time. My wife never…"

He shook his head and Lilly could hear both the sadness and the bitterness in his voice.

"I'd like a favor," Soledad said, sensing the subject might best be changed. "I don't really care what you tell the sheriff about all this. All I ask is that you tell him we drove off in a blue van and you heard us say something about us heading to Denver."

"Sure, I can do that. I'll give you time to get down to the highway before I call."

Soledad held out his hand. "Thanks, Mr.Catanach."

The old rancher took his hand with a firm grip, shook it, and turned to Lilly. "Give her some rein, but best you keep her close, too" he said.

"I'll do that," Lilly replied, smiled, and turned to the truck.

As soon as they cleared Villa Grove, Soledad took out his cell phone and punched in a number. For some reason, he put the call on speaker, and they listened to it ring for a dozen or so times before Mariposa answered.

"Harris Solar Energy. How may I help you?"

"Mariposa. It's Jaime. I should tell you that there's no longer any need to answer that way."

"Very well, but you might be interested to know a woman called earlier this evening. I took her number."

"Well, Harris Solar is no longer in business. Look, we're going to need your assistance. We've got what we came for and we're heading south. We need that plane again."

"How soon? It might take a little time to arrange."

"Here's the thing. We need to get to…" He paused. "We're not going back to Houston. We need to go home. ¿Lo *entiendes?* The problem is one of us doesn't have a passport or an ID. So, wherever you have us going, it'll have to be a place where we don't have to deal with *La Migra*. ¿*Sí?*"

"*Sí*. I understand."

"I'm thinking we'll be in Albuquerque in maybe five hours. Let me know if that's a possibility. How about our truck?"

"Don't worry. All will be taken care of. I will call you as soon as I know something," Mariposa said, and abruptly disconnected.

"How's your arm?" Lilly asked Kate. They had paused at the highway turn off just long enough to retrieve the first aid kit from the back of the truck and wrap Kate's arm with a roll of gauze.

"Who are you people?" Kate asked, ignoring the question. It was the first thing she had said to them since leaving Catanach's house.

"I told you. Hattie sent us," Lilly answered.

"You're friends of hers?"

"Not exactly," Soledad replied. "You heard me say that we're not taking you to Houston. Your grandmother's waiting for you in Mexico City."

"Mexico City. Why there?"

What the hell, Lilly thought. Kate deserved to know why. It might give her time to digest just what might lie ahead. It wasn't her place though to fill in the blanks. That would be up to Hattie.

"Your grandfather lives there," she said.

Kate shot her a look that was impossible to interpret in the dim interior of the truck's cab. "I don't know my… I don't have a grandfather," she said, the confusion in her voice obvious.

"You do now." Lilly placed her hand on Kate's leg. I bet you'll like him. Let's just say, he's an interesting man. I have to ask you. How did Leroy take it?"

Kate grunted in what might have been disappointment mixed with annoyance. "I don't know what I was thinking. Being with him, I mean. Running off like this."

"Do you think you're the only woman who's ever been taken in by a smile and a cheap line of bullshit?"

"I want you to know that I've got better sense," Kate said. "Or at least I thought I did. Do you know what that asshole asked me after I told him it was over? He wanted me to ask you if he could have more of the money."

"Oh, well. What do they say? Men are like dogs. Sooner or later, they all bark."

Soledad made an attempt at a barking sound, but neither of the two women found it in them to laugh.

"Okay, ladies," he said after a moment had passed. "I'm thinking breakfast burritos in Albuquerque. Lilly, find us some music and let's roll."

MEXICO CITY

Six Weeks Later

Lilly arranged to meet Kate for coffee at Café Nin, a coffee house a ten-minute walk from Lilly's apartment. Because Lilly was a regular, she managed to reserve a table on the narrow side-patio.

There had been an intense, but brief thunderstorm an hour before, and the air was still laden with the rich bouquet of wet streets, ozone, and the intense perfume wafting down from the morning glories that trailed from the trellis above.

Kate was fashionably late. The vice of the young, Lilly allowed. She found the ease in which Kate had settled into her new circumstances to be praiseworthy if not disconcerting on some level. She had to accept that Kate's free-wheeling, laissez-faire attitude was just another trait of the young and unencumbered. Kate had earned a modicum of independence after what she had been through. What had been Luther Catanach's advice? Give her some rein but also keep her close. Hattie had been of the same persuasion despite Jeronimo's opposite inclination to forgo loosening any reins just yet.

Kate's appearance in the entrance to the patio interrupted her thoughts. At first, Lilly hardly recognized her, for Kate had cut her hair into a short bob and dyed it platinum blonde. She wore the perquisite torn jeans and a cream-colored, diaphanous peasant blouse.

"Hola, Chica," Lilly said and waved her over.

They exchanged kisses. They had hardly settled into their seats before Kate dug into her large leather handbag and pulled out a palm-sized dark green packet with the word Mexico embossed in gold on the front. Lilly immediately recognized it as a Mexican passport.

"What do you think?" Kate asked, flipping it open and holding it out for Lilly's inspection.

"Jeronimo didn't waste any time," Lilly said, leaning closer to read it. "Catalina Hermosa." She grunted in appreciation. "I like it, but it's too bad the photo isn't up to date. And your birthplace. Isla de Mujeres? At least that's original. You're lucky. He had them put Juarez on mine. It made it sound like I was born in some border town brothel."

"You've got a false passport, too?" Kate asked in surprise as she tucked the passport back into her bag.

"You've heard everyone call me Lila. Well, my real name is Lilly DeFranco."

"I'm guessing there's some reason you had to change your name and get a new passport."

The waiter came before Lilly could reply. They ordered espressos and a chocolate croissant for Kate.

"It's…. *Un cuento Chino.*" Lilly said after the waiter walked off.

"Wait. What? A Chinese…*cuento?* I don't know that word."

"A Chinese story. It means a long story. One night soon after I began working for your grandfather, he let the tequila talk for him and he opened up and told me a lot about himself. You know how he got to where he's at. He called his life that. A Chinese story. What he meant was his life had been one with lots of blind curves and unexpected developments. When I think about it, that's maybe not a bad way to live your life."

"But do you mind if I ask you why? I mean the alias?"

"There are things about my past. Criminal stuff," she added after a moment's hesitation.

At times, her past had always seemed to crowd out who she felt she really was. Her time here in Mexico City had started to reform that image of herself, but the recent foray to rescue Kate had resurrected certain demons and memories that made her realize her dark side was never far below the water line of her psyche. She still struggled to believe she had made peace with that part of herself.

"A story for another time" she said. "How are the Spanish lessons coming?" she asked in an obvious attempt to change the subject.

"*Muy bien.* But the fucking tenses are killing me."

"Watch all the *telenovelas* and stupid game shows you can stand. And just stand around on the street and listen. That's what I did."

"Yeah, but Jeronimo wants me to start at the university in fall. He's pulled all these strings to get me enrolled."

"What's the hurry? If you're not ready, you start the next semester. Tell me something. How's Hattie doing with all Jeronimo's meddling?"

"You know that she's flying back to Houston tomorrow. I think she needs a break from it all. But I'm betting she'll be back sooner than expected. If you ask me, I think they're sleeping together."

"What do you mean? Like there's something going on between the two of them? You can't mean romance?"

Kate shrugged. "All I'll say is I hear their doors opening and closing in the middle of the night."

"*Cabra viejo,*" Lilly muttered softly.

"And the way they look at each other. And the way they tease each other. Mostly about Hattie's shaved head. It won't surprise me if she starts letting it grow out."

"Jeronimo could use some romance. They both could."

"Speaking of romance. What's the deal with you and Jaime? I thought you said you were moving back to the States."

Lilly shrugged. "Undecided. I'm still a bit nervous about going there. You know, because of some old legal issues. Even with my Mexican passport, I can't take the chance someone is going to check my fingerprints. Jeronimo thinks if he throws enough money at someone that all my records will magically disappear. You can't bribe a computer though. I used to have a friend who could help, but that was in a different life."

She found herself thinking of Harlan Quist and wondered what had become of him. They sipped their espressos in silence and listened to the distant thunder. She looked at Kate and felt a pang of… What? Envy? Or was it perhaps just some vague melancholia stemming from the lingering uncertainty she felt about her own unsettled situation?

"You know you don't always get second chances," she offered after a moment had passed.

Kate looked at her and nodded, her face suddenly somber. "You're worried I'll blow it, aren't you? Hattie worries about that, too. She says I can't let what happened in the past define me is how she puts it. That I need to let in the light. That makes it easier to make the right choices. Walk the right path. All that Buddhist stuff."

Lilly nodded. "She's right. But sometimes you don't always get to make choices. There are times when circumstances make them for you. Remember that."

Kate studied her for a moment before reaching across the table and taking Lilly's hand. They held each other's hands, their intimacy interrupted by a loud peal of thunder.

"How much longer are you going to live at Jeronimo's?" Lilly asked impulsively. "I mean there's an opening in my building. Top floor, too. It has a garden patio. You can even see the castle from there."

"Yeah? We could be neighbors," Kate offered, her face brightening. "I think I'd like that." Kate glanced down at her cell phone as it chirped a message. "That's my tutor. I forgot to tell him I'd be late. I have to go. So, will I see you at Jeronimo's tonight for Hattie's farewell dinner?"

"Sure." They kissed and Kate hurried out.

She signaled at the waiter as she picked at the remains of Kate's croissant. As she rummaged for some pesos in the small backpack that doubled as her purse, she happened across the notecard Hattie had given her soon after she and Soledad had safely delivered Kate. It was a pale, rose-colored card of expensive-looking, handmade stationary, French according to the watermark on the back. Hattie had expressed her heartfelt gratitude for what they had done. At the bottom, she had written a quote from Henry Miller.

"One's destination is never a place, but a new way of seeing things."

She smiled as she read the quote a second time. She counted out some pesos and stood to leave just as Soledad appeared.

"This is a surprise," she said, settling back in her chair. "How did you know I was here?"

"Did you forget? You told me this morning you were meeting Kate here," he said, dropping into the other chair.

They looked at each other for a moment before Soledad broke the silence. "Jeronimo wants me to go to Houston and settle some business. You want to come along?" When she didn't reply right away, he went on. "He mentioned that he'd offered you a job there. I thought you might want to go there and check it out."

She surprised herself when she replied, "I'm not taking the job."

He raised his eyebrows, his face registering his own surprise. "Why not? I thought..."

She quickly reached across the table and placed her fingers on his lips, preventing him from saying more.

"No more of this thinking shit. I realized there's no point in plotting out my life. It was beginning to seem like some cheap novel." *Un cuento Chino,* she thought.

Hattie was right. Let in some light and let it become what it is.

He offered her a look of confusion. "When did you change your mind?"

'I don't know. Five minutes ago."

He reached over, took her hand, but didn't say anything.

"I realized that for the first time in my life, I have a family. Kate, Jeronimo, Hattie. You. I'm done running. But you have to know that I don't do this very well. Staying, I mean."

The waiter returned. "*¿Más café?*

"*Si, por favor. ¿Tienes galletas de boda?*" she asked.

"*Si.*" The waiter replied and walked off.

"Wedding cookies? Are you proposing?" Soledad asked with a smile.

"God no! Those cookies are just good with coffee. Look," she said, leaning across the table and taking his hand. "Just don't make me run. Promise me that."

"If you run, I'll be running with you."

It thundered again; this time closer.

"I think maybe we should go and beat the storm."

"It won't last long. You want to just move inside?"

"Come to think of it, I may have left my windows open. Why don't we see if we can get our coffee and cookies to go?"

Soledad shrugged. "Yeah, I guess we could."

"How about if I told you I have half and half at home?"

"In that case, I say let's hurry. How about I go pay up and get our coffee and cookies, and you go and flag us down a taxi? I'll meet you out front."

Lilly made her way out to the street and stood waiting at the curb for a taxi to appear. She absently watched the traffic pass by and thought about what she had told Soledad about running. Who was it that had told her that running was what outlaws always ended up doing? Had it been Harlan? Running had been her *modus operandi* for most of her life. More often than not it meant running away from something rather than toward something. This time she decided she would run toward something.

There was another loud peal of thunder, and she could now smell the approaching rain. At any moment, she expected the skies to open. An omen, perhaps? She thought of something Hilario had once told her as they sat waiting in the car for a rainstorm to pass. *"Tláloc nos llama al cuerto cielo. Al paraíso'"* he had said somberly as a bolt of lightning struck especially close by.

Tláloc. The Aztec god of rain and the fourth heaven. She remembered one of the stone deities in Jeronimo's solarium depicted *Tláloc.* The fourth heaven. *El paraíso*, she thought, glancing up at the darkening sky. Was that what this was? *Tláloc* calling us to paradise?

She saw a taxi switch lanes down the block and began waving.

THE END